SERIES

MEDITERRANEAN PRIVATE EYE

MANHUNT IN PARADISE

FEATURING

THE PIPS

IN

MEDITERRANEAN

PRIVATE EYE

SERIES

BY

JOHN ALAN ANDREWS

Copyright © 2024 by John A. Andrews

Books That Will Enhance Your Life

ISBN: 9798328370042

Cover Art: ALI

Cover Photo: ALI

All rights reserved.

MANHUNT

IN PARADISE

BODY

IN A SUITCASE

THE THUMB DRIVES

MANHUNT IN PARADISE

TABLE OF CONTENTS

CHAPTER ONE..8
CHAPTER TWO..13
CHAPTER THREE..18
CHAPTER FOUR...23
CHAPTER FIVE...27
CHAPTER SIX..31
CHAPTER SEVEN..35
CHAPTER EIGHT..40
CHAPTER NINE...47
CHAPTER TEN..50
CHAPTER ELEVEN...53
CHAPTER TWELVE...56
CHAPTER THIRTEEN...60
CHAPTER FOURTEEN...64
CHAPTER FIFTEEN..67
CHAPTER SIXTEEN..70
CHAPTER SEVENTEEN..75
CHAPTER EIGHTEEN...78
CHAPTER NINETEEN...80
CHAPTER TWENTY...82
CHAPTER TWENTY-ONE...85
CHAPTER TWENTY-TWO...87
CHAPTER TWENTY-THREE...90
CHAPTER TWENTY-FOUR..93
CHAPTER TWENTY-FIVE..96
CHAPTER TWENTY-SIX..100
CHAPTER TWENTY-SEVEN..103
CHAPTER TWENTY-EIGHT..108
CHAPTER TWENTY-NINE...110

CHAPTER ONE

NICE rests on the Mediterranean. It is paradisical, or what some may categorize as a Nice city in France, set on the French Riveria. It nurtures a paradisical view of ports teetering with orange roofs and villas set in mostly ancient architecture.

It is early mid-morning. An Air France commercial jet gradually descends from clear skies and lands at Nice Cote d'Azur Airport.

Its passengers rush to the baggage claim to retrieve

their luggage. Based on the angle, only their lower portions are visible. Additionally, their upper torso or faces aren't disclosed.

Without a luggage glitch, they head for the exit, except for two passengers, a man and a woman dressed in boots and denim attire. Across the way, a fully lit Mediterranean Bank peaks.

They stroll towards the Bank. Subsequently, a set of mobile female feet linger. The male Persona briskly walks inside the Bank and up to the teller's window. His backside dominates. The Bank Teller's masculine-looking hands count a hefty sum of Euros and USD.

The male Persona's right hand points the gun at the Teller after the Teller's hands over sums of cash. Five ONE round cut down the Teller — the Personas who entered and robbed the Bank leg it without a trace.

Tram wheels squeal amid loud tooting tram horns. , The tram with the AEROPORT sign at the brow rolls into the terminal and flaunts destination Terminal #2 along its station. The tram's PA System announces - Terminal Un! Rush hour Passengers de-train, most toting to-be-checked luggage and carry-ons in droves and vice versa.

A kid on a leach sucking on a candy cane and exiting gets in the way of exiting tram passengers. His mother reins him in and out of harm's way.

A strong presence man-on-a-mission BILLY BLACK, 50s, bald, African American wearing a tan trench coat pushes clustered commuters aside through another tram door. He hustles toward the terminal unchallenged.

A Gen Z REDHEAD GIRL, aka Corie Phelps, traverses with her iPhone pressed against her ear, almost in a head-on collision with Billy Black. He is slowed momentarily while avoiding that accident.

"Excuse me, Madam! Police business!"

"Bonjour! Bonjour!"

Greetings from the Redhead Girl.

In the meantime, she captures his profile with her cell phone and yells:

"You are too late! Typical Cops! They show up after the fox has left the barn... with the sheep."

Billy Black ignores her shenanigans and embraces the distance. He darts inside Terminal #1.

Simultaneously, YOVANDA NICHOLS, in her 40s, with braided hair and Nigerian descent, emerges from the next crowded tram car. Her model physique earns her a collection of male whistles. Trailing behind Billy Black, she jets. Seers clear the way for the Diva.

"Let us move it, guys! Are you getting on, off, or out of the way?"

She hustles.

ALFRED NOBLES, aka AL, is an Irish man in his mid-50s who sports a dark trench coat. His accessories comprise dark-tint mini horn-rimmed glasses, a fat tobacco pipe hanging from his mouth, a beret hat, mini spectacles, and a busy mini binocular camera. Paparazzi-like, he captures everything in sight, annoying passengers glued to their gadgets and platform antics.

Sirens crescendo over loud human chatter and radio noise.

"Fatalities? Where is he?"

Al Nobles asks a boarding passenger entering the platform.

He doesn't respond. Typical French culture is like it's none of his business – I see no evil and hear no evil. Plus, I only speak French.

Al Nobles eludes him and maneuvers inside the Terminal.

The PIPS keep coming like a pack of wolves released from the woodland.

VINCE TAYLOR, in his 50s, is camera-ready, with a neatly shaved mustache under a black Stingy Brim Fedora hat. He is in a deficit step, attempting to catch up with the others.

Racing ahead of Taylor, Al Nobles says under his breath:

"Does nobody know anything?"

Passengers, as if by choice, hibernate in their worlds – Whatever is going on has nothing to do with me.

In addition, MADISON ALLEN, in her 50s, is collecting data on her iPad. With the tram in the background, she enters the Terminal in cataloging mode.

"Culprits at large? No Security? What else is amiss? This is the darn airport, for Heaven's sake. Get a grip on something – anything!"

Meanwhile, playing massive-catch-up with a feminine swagger is RALPH GOMEZ, 30s. He hits the Terminal grounds with an attitude – this world is mine, and we are The Pips.

"Guys, there is nowhere in Paradise he can hide. He could still be inside Terminal One. Let's move it!"

He adjusts the volume on his handheld radio, which is transmitting massive static. That same hand totes his treasured makeup kit.

CHAPTER TWO

The Pips are resolute, garnering evidence from the yellow-taped protected crime scene.
"Nothing surprises me! Not since Russia invaded Ukraine."
Says Billy Black.
An ONLOOKER inside the crowded Terminal evolves, buzzing with human chatter and chants:
"Hip, Hip, hooray! The Pips are here! What are you going to do…?"

Billy Black traverses. He is mission-bound. The particeps criminis are missing.

A static-laden Radio transmits in French.

French Police emerge, swarming the crime scene. An Investigator emerges from their ranks. He almost trips on the five 9mm shells scattered on the floor. Poised, he reviews and collects items into evidence.

Billy Black gets a CU of the Bank's interior through its glass-structured foreground. It is grotesque. He looks away from the bloody corpse, still pumping blood.

It is now an investigative frenzy. Airport Security busily plays catch up, pressing the huddled Pips, seeking answers. Billy Black locks eyes with an Airport Security Officer.

"Has anyone claimed responsibility?"

Asks Billy Black.

"No!"

Says that stapled Onlooker.

"It wasn't me!

Says an Airport Security Officer

"That is lame, Officer."

Says Billy Black.

"What is lame?"

Asks the Airport Security Officer.

"Your answer. Someone has been killed. What happened to your surveillance? Give us the footage."

States, Billy Black.

Pointing at two Uniformed Workers emerging with a ladder destined for monitoring bank cameras. The Airport Security Officer says:

"Ask those guys."

Billy Black does amidst their defenses.

"What happened?"

"Camera malfunctioned? Inside job?"

They ask themselves.

Billy Black interjects.

"Let us not jump to conclusions. Which way did the killers go?"

Security Officer, unsure of killer's locality – shush. Billy Black turns to his team. A French Police INVESTIGATOR WELCH intervenes while continuing to secure the crime scene with additional yellow tape. He eyes Billy Black, alleging his possible domination of the robbery-murder case.

"Hey, Black, it has become apparent that you and your guys bit off more than you can chew on this one."

Billy Black stayed.

"Moving forward, We've got this..."

The Airport Security Officer states:

"You might have zeal but lack..."
Investigator Welch interrupts,
"Someone once said: Fools rush where wise men fear to tread."
Billy Black answers:
"And another warning: It is not the size of the dog in the fight but the size of the fight in the dog."
Billy Black walks away from the war of words and indulges his team.
He strides toward the train tram's platform. The Pips follow in tow.
"What is wrong with those guys? I do not get it. Something smells! "
Yovanda Nichols says they are challenged as the rest of The Pips land on the platform.
The Redhead Girl enthusiastically points across the parking lot.
"Look! We lost them. They must have carjacked a burgundy car and drove west...Too Late!"
In the backdrop, Al Nobles is absorbed, documenting the crime scene.
BILLY BLACK hears the Redhead Girl's observation and races in her direction. He asks:
"Where did he go? What does he look like?"
"Caucasian! Pony-tailed hair. I have pictures. It happened suddenly!"
"And the woman?"

Asks Yovanda Nichols.

"A Super Model. Also, I have flicks of her."

"Can your airdrop - facilitate?"

Asks Billy Black, anticipating a photo drop. Redhead Girl declines.

Adding to the travesty, tooting trams arrive, blocking crosswalk access and eye level connecting to the other side where the gunman's alleged carjacking befell.

Ralph Gomez says to Corrie Phelps,

"If you see him again, call us."

"Ghostbusters?"

She asks, in jest.

"We are The PIPS!"

Says Gomez.

She smiles.

Billy Black gives her thumbs up. The Redhead Girl boards a tram. It motors off. The Pips walk across the tracks where the bandits made their getaway and board a waiting passenger van. It carts them away.

Police, Patrol Cars, Dogs, Eavesdroppers, Flight Crew, Passengers, Personnel, and sign: I HEART NICE - backdrops.

CHAPTER THREE

Investigator Welch walks through the front door to his Cul-de-sac home. Yawning excessively and being physically drained seems an understatement. He has had better days revised by the award for Cop of The Week 2023 hanging on the wall.
Welch removes his jacket and hangs it in the nearby coat closet. He yawns again, wilder and woolier.

Noticeably, one gun strapped to his pants leg, one to his shoulder holster, and the other to the holster of his belt.

Welch removes his weapons and noisily lays them on the kitchen table. To him, this has become a rut.

He moseys to an adjacent refrigerator, opens it, and retrieves a "Kro" 1664 beer bottle. Judging by his craving look, it's his favorite.

He twists off the cork and tosses the stopper in the trash can underneath the sink. He strolls to the Living room with the craved brew.

Welch takes another swig, burps, and plops down on the recliner. He searches for and finds the remote beneath the cushion. He cuts on the TV.

Welch takes another swig of the brew and sinks into the recliner. Now glued to the "One-eyed-monster," an Old School TV Ad campaign fades out.

Breaking News pops onto the lower thirds of the TV screen: Identity of Nice Killer Revealed.

Welch, to himself.

"It is about time! Our guys caught him, I am sure. Yes?"

"We continued to follow the dilemma early this morning at Nice Airport. According to sources, the identity of the bank teller who suffered multiple bullet wounds to his chest and died as a result has been identified as Malcolm Yates. According to sources, Yates' banking tenure lasted for a decade.

Meanwhile, his alleged killer or killers are still at large. Sources claim that the alleged one-man and one-woman team fled the scene in a burgundy carjacked automobile after the killing of Yates. We will continue to update you on this moving story. Now, back to our regularly scheduled program.

The regularly scheduled program rolls on: This is an old Western flick. The horse gallops and kicks off its rider. He falls hard to the ground.

"They didn't? Darn! What a fumble…He can run, but he can't hide. He's not in France. Stay in the hunt, Gendarmerie!"

The horse keeps galloping along. Dust trails…

Welch takes multiple guzzles of his "Kro". He downs it, ambles the kitchen, and fetches another beer. He struts back to the Living Room with his beer in hand. He stands, distancing himself from the comfortable recliner.

Welch, matter-of-factly:

"You can't ride a horse if you don't know much about a horse. Get off. Why get on one? Darn fool. You should know that. Common sense…"

Welch, to himself:

"I thought poster boy Billy Black and his Peeps would have caught those bastards. It is our show, Black! You fail to realize that you're nothing but small Minnows in a big pond. No swag, no sway. You'll be swimming around forever."

Welch is enjoying his second beer.

The cell phone rings.

Unwillingly, Welch takes the call. He would instead finish the beer, though.

"Officer Welch, this is the Dispatch unit. Someone just called in, claiming the lights on your cruiser have been on for the last fifteen minutes. Are you aware of such?"

Asks a nonchalant FRENCH POLICE DISPATCHER.

Welch, agitated.

"Darn! Hold on, I'll check on it."

Welch strolls to the kitchen table and rummages. He does not find what he's looking for. He goes to the closet and checks his coat pockets. He finds the car remote, returns to the front door, disarms the lights, and returns inside.

Welch, into the phone,

"Thanks, guys. Got it."

French Police Dispatcher responds,

"You are welcome. Stay safe, Officer Welch."

Welch closes the door. He arms the deadbolt lock on his front door and double-checks the lock for certainty. Satisfied. He returns to his beer. The beer bottle almost topples with that move, but he recovers and downs it.

Subsequently, his insobriety is evident. He treks to the bedroom, gingerly and rickety.

CHAPTER FOUR

Mission-bound Billy Black navigates the streets of Nice with candor. He runs into road blockades and checkpoints orchestrated by French Police. On the dashboard, a printed, lettered sign reads The PIPS. Check Pointers, take notice. He clears breezily and speeds away along the Nice coast.
Up ahead. A Gas Station signal peaks.

Billy Black arrives and pulls up at the gas pump. He steps out. Peripherally, his eye catches a hind shot of MOTORIST #1 set to board the vehicle.

Billy Black waves to the Motorist and gets his attention before the man closes the door.

"Bonjour!"

Shouts, Billy Black.

Motorist #1 waves in response. He's rushed.

"My name is Billy Black with the Pips…"

Motorist #1 accommodates.

"I have heard about you, the Pips. The new guys are on the block. Not sure we need more police. What we need is more benefits for seniors."

"Investigations …the "I" in Pips. That is what we do for Southern France."

"Really?"

Asks, Motorist #1.

Billy Black moves into his space.

"Sir, a Bank Teller was murdered in Nice. I am in search of that shooter, on the run. He is at least six feet, wears a ponytail, and could be accompanied by a woman who looks like a model. Any information you can provide would be greatly appreciated."

"Sorry. He has not crossed my path. Not sure he will. The woman with him? How do we know she is not responsible for the murder?"

"It was alleged that his biometrics was lifted from those bullet shell casings recovered at the crime scene."
"...and Hers?"
Asks, Motorist #1.
"Not sure if hers were planted at the crime scene."
States, Billy Black.
"Interesting twist? She did not touch anything. Not even the furniture?"
Says, Motorist #1.
"Once again, no findings so far. Please do not quote me; DNA could reveal her presence at the scene."
Says Billy Black.
"FYI, this ponytail hairstyle is quite common for most men in Southern France."
Says, Motorist #1.
Billy Black reaches for his phone and shows the Motorist a picture of the alleged murderer.
"Once again, he has not crossed my path. Ask someone else. I've got to go. You know, family stuff. I have a full house to run. The wife, her mother, the kids, and the dogs are about to adopt a stray cat. Plus, I sensed you judged me by my ponytail. Mistaken identity... ha-ha! It wasn't me, Officer Black."
Says, Motorist #1.
"So said Shaggy..."

"Very funny. Mr. Black, I hope you find your man. You must understand: Every ponytail-hairstyle-wearing man did not shoot that bank teller in Nice. It was a tragedy. Very unusual on the Coast. Nice try, though. You are throwing minnows to catch sharks."

Billy Black hands the Motorist his business card.

"If you see him, reach out."

"You earn a fat bonus on his capture. Don't you? How much do you get? This is France."

"We just need to catch him before he strikes again. Merci."

Motorist #1 nods YES and gets inside his car. It motors off.

Billy Black hustles toward his car, and en route, he runs into MOTORIST #2, who is about to pump gas in an upscale Mercedes Benz.

CHAPTER FIVE

This Motorist #2, oblivious to Billy Black, had been eavesdropping on the recent conversation between Motorist #1 and himself.
Rehearsed:
"It wasn't me, either. The Man is still on the loose, huh? What is the story about his girlfriend - the girl? Silent and complicated? She must be. Did he kidnap her or did she him? Did she travel with him

voluntarily? Is it a fact that her biometrics were not present at the crime scene? It sounds like this case of yours is saturated with evidence tampering, fixers, and double-crossers on a higher level. Why did you choose such a case, Mr. Black?"

"We are still gathering the facts as we speak. Not much to go on. The case is still young. Someone pulled the trigger and shot a Bank Teller in Nice. If your friends know whodunit, let us know."

"Make me a decent offer. I'll help you loosen up the case. Give it good legs to stand on."

"Thanks. We have already assembled a team of investigators. Will find the underlying cause of it, eventually."

States, Billy Black.

Motorist #2 eyes widen.

"Another hand would not hurt. It seems like John Shaft or Colombo; you are stuck with many probabilities. "

He continues,

"You need help reading those tea leaves, Mr. Black. Why not close the case sooner than later? Find the killer or killers. Bring them to justice. So, parents in Paradise can cease the ordeal of reigning in their kids early, and the citizens of this area can return to their normal lives."

Billy Black has earned himself an earful and is ready to depart.

"This whole search has upended not only our tourism but our lifestyle. We have never inherited such a drought in tourism. Ask Booking.com or research their analytic metric.
"We will catch him. Thanks for your indulgence, anyway."
Billy Black confirms.
"Billy Black, I'm very resourceful. You must understand. They don't come any better than the who is who in the region."
A line of cars behind Billy Black's car lengthens. Most laden with venting FRUSTRATED MOTORISTS.
They yell:
"Come on! Let's move it! Cops! Cops! Cops, and more darn Cops!"
HORNS TOOT LOUDLY
Motorist #2 points to the growing convoy of venting motorists and smirks.
Billy Black looks in the direction of those motorists. A radical tether on vandalizing his vehicle, Billy Black caresses his holstered weapon in an "I dare you" stance.
Motorist #2 whimpers,
"See. You planted this darn thorn inside our flesh. An unsolved case of bottlenecks in a traffic mayhem, and beyond."
Those attack motorists back off.

Billy Black gets it,
"Thanks."
"Yep. Fool me once you don't fool me twice. This situation bothers me. Happy trails! You'll be hunting me down to strike a deal before you find your man! Be sure you have my fee. Plus, a bonus for your stalling.
Billy Black, watching his back, bounces.
Billy Black, under his breath,
"Your BS? So rancid. It ferments. Smells like cat vomit."
Billy Black arrives at his car. He boards hastily but with caution and eyeing them peripherally.

CHAPTER SIX

Up Ahead. Traffic bottlenecks are extensive.
Motorist #2 car trails Billy Black's, immersed in that traffic flow.
Oblivious to Billy Black though, MOTORIST #3 and MOTORIST #4, both wearing pony-tailed hairstyles like that worn by the alleged killer at Nice Airport,

noses. These two Frenchmen in their 50s are having a phone pow-wow on their phones, both driver windows are partially cracked.

Eavesdropping, on this deep discussion across the way from behind two adjacent gas pumps. Body language says: Billy Black does not score high marks in their POV.

Motorist #3 asks,

"What is that investigator's MO? Drugs, Sex, or Rock and Roll?"

"To catch the alleged killer and his accomplice. The two engaged in the Bank robbery."

Responds, Motorist #4.

"Are you sure? No one knows who pulled the trigger for sure. Yes?"

Motorist #3 asks.

"True."

Motorist #3 states,

"What's his name?"

Motorist #4 asks and continues,

"The Investigator?"

"Yep. The cop, blackness? His name has recently been dominating the news in Paris, and Southern France. It looks like he had a pistol in his waist while talking with those two motorists. They seem to have brushed him off. It is a legal dilemma Cops are known to get trigger-happy on a dime."

Says Motorist #3.

Motorist #4 responds,

"His name is Billy Black. As far as we know, he is American and helms the investigative group - The Pips... It seems he has an appetite for selective fact-finding. You notice he didn't even approach us regarding his case, one of such magnitude.

"Motorist #3 says candidly,

"He didn't."

"Billy Black should know if he's going to be of significance in our city. He should at least start by reading our local paper to find out who is who."

Says, Motorist #4.

"He's talking with straw men instead of the pillars of this community who can give legs to the case. He should know you can't make chicken soup out of chicken shit or fight no war with Toy Soldiers on the ground."

Says, Motorist #3.

He lights up a cigarette, takes a puff, and continues: "Who are these killers? I mean, what are their names? Nobody knows. It's almost 24 hours since they reopened the terminal. Zip, Nothing, Nada! What if they are homegrown? This gig-saw puzzle seems to be missing a few pieces."

Motorist #4 responds,

"Well said, Dobbs. Darn, so far, he doesn't even know whodunit."

Yellow Jackets groupies assemble, seemingly minding their own business.

Motorist #4 is over the top:

"Are those Yellow Jackets involved?"

"Not sure if they are starting an unrelated demonstration. So, how are we supposed to know who shot that bank teller?"

States, Motorist #3.

Motorist #4 responds,

"Billy Black is not Frenchie... He's Yankee."

Motorist #3 states,

"Pas de francais."

Motorist #4 responds,

"Oui."

"If he should even attempt to question me, as to if I saw or didn't see his man? I'm sticking to my guns - I did not see your man!"

Says, Motorist #3 resolutely.

CHAPTER SEVEN

Billy Black jumps in his auto. It motors off, leaving both motorists in its wind and smoke.
"He's gone. Have a nice life. I mean a Nice life."
Says, Motorist #4.
INTERCUTING between Billy Black inside his speed mobile, Motorist #3 and Motorist #4 parked in their respective vehicle and gazing in the direction of Billy Black's exit.

"I thought he was building his case on every driver's input. Did he just leave?"
Asks, Motorist #3.
"Oui."
"Ses affaires puent."
Responds, Motorist #3
"Rance."
Motorist #3 responds,
"It seems Welch is taking a back seat on this one. Can't have this one be like a cog in the wheel impeding Francois Welch's promotion. Two months to go, right?"
"Yep. Welch earns it. About this Billy Black? If all else fails, like a mah-jongg player we have Propaganda inside our tool kit. Don't play us, Billy Black. We'll go to Russia, full blast Putin, and the Kremlin on you."
Music from inside Billy Black's auto crescendo. He sways to the beat, and his car careens. Suddenly, the music fades.
The Radio Announcer interjects,
"This is a special news break. According to sources we have learned that the bank teller killed in the bank robbery at Nice Cote d'Azur airport this morning has been identified as Malcolm Yates. Once again, the victim in the Nice Airport shooting has been identified as Malcolm Yates. Additionally, that

is all we have for now. More to come on this unfolding story."

"Come on guys! That's stale news. When is someone going to address motive, and the entities suppressing discovery? Who claimed responsibility? There are too many big fish in this small pond."

Billy Black says, as his car swerves out of an almost fender-bender. His auto peels away rear-viewing multiple vehicles and leaving them in the dust.

The road ahead is suddenly a clear path.

Suddenly. Up Ahead. On the road's shoulder, a cloud of steam emits from underneath the hood of a parked vehicle.

His auto gears down, pull over and park at a safe distance ahead of the smoking vehicle.

It is abandoned.

Smoke from the hood strengthens.

Billy Black rubs his itching nose.

He pops his auto's trunk. He retrieves a fire extinguisher and pickaxe.

He is mission-bound, and races toward the smoking vehicle, rubbing his nose.

The vehicle is the replica of the carjacked runaway burgundy automobile described by The Redhead Girl at Nice Airport. Billy Black clues in - the same car.

Billy Black pries the passenger door open using a pickaxe. Limited visibility prevails. He uses the fire extinguisher. The fire subsides. He investigates. There are no occupants.

He eyes the glove compartment. He tugs on it.

It is LOCKED.

Dense SMOKE RISES

He resourcefully extinguishes the rising steam.

He PRIES the compartment open.

Steam residue lags.

He tugs at it hard. It flies open. Inside. There is a mini flashlight. He cuts it on.

Billy Black notices two train tickets. Aided by the flashlight, he sees the departure time printed on both noon from Gare De Nice Ville. His breasts pocket secures them. He glances at his watch, focused.

On Billy Black's timepiece, it reads 11:00 AM.

Tension mounts. A mission-impossible scenario brews with explosive consequences. He pops the trunk's release button from inside the glove compartment. The trunk opens dominated by smoke.

With the pickaxe in one hand. Fire extinguisher in the next and the flashlight in his mouth, he darts toward the trunk.

Steam simmers. He rummages inside, notices, and recovers a pony-tailed hairstyle wig. Plus, two pairs of fake beards, mustaches, and eyebrows. Steam intensifies.

A manila envelope peaks. He grabs the envelope and rips it open. He finds pictures of the robbed Bank's interior. Plus, hand-drawn sketches of bank teller, Malcolm Yates. He bounces with the preponderance of evidence.

Billy Black arrives at his car, and darts inside.
ENGINE CUTS ON
TIRES SQUEAL
AUTO MOTORS OFF SPEEDILY.

CHAPTER EIGHT

Billy Black accesses the radio on the passenger seat and seeks a signal. It transmits muffled. Finally, a clear signal appears.
"Calling all Pips. Report to headquarters immediately and be prepared for a trip to Monaco on the noon train.
Al Nobles responds,
"Is our man in Monaco?"

"It seems like he could be heading there soon, hurry."

Responds, Billy Black.

A bomb-like blast erupts. The abandoned vehicle explodes, heaving smoke, fire, and debris into the atmosphere. Billy Black's auto speedily clears out.

Billy Black focusing on revenge:

"The Pips are coming for you! What are you going to do, when they corner you, eh?"

Across the way. The Militaries immediately patrol the side streets in search of perpetrators.

Moments later. Billy Black arrives at The Pips Headquarters. He finds the rest of The Pips assembled. However, there is no Redhead Girl. Their eyes scan the room in wonderment.

Suddenly, the Redhead barges in, toting two tennis rackets inside a racket holder. She is breathless.

"Sorry, I am late, guys. I was at the train station earlier and saw someone who looked just like our man. Except, there was no ponytail hairstyle, he looked aged, without his accomplice."

"Any proof?"

Asks, Madison Allen.

"I followed my intuition and captured multiple flicks."

Redhead Girl shares her flicks with the team.

Billy Black mediates,

"Interesting pics! That is a strong possibility this is our man.
(pause)
Miss Phelps, welcome to the team. Thanks again for helping us get underneath this one. Adding these pillars to our case, brainwashing has no place to dwell."
Billy Black retrieves a bouquet from Ralph Gomez and presents it to Phelps. Surprised and flattered, she admires the gift. Subsequently, her face reddens as she tears up.
Billy Black courteously,
"Corrie Phelps, welcome to the PIPS!"
"Mr. Black, and The Pips' team... I am so honored to be part of your elite squad."
States, Redhead Girl with a smile.
The rest of the Pips applaud amid Phelps' tear-shed moment.
Al Nobles, sensing the bonding between The Redhead Girl and Ralph Gomez, zeros in on Ralph Gomez.
"Pretty flowers."
"Thanks. Kudos to the man at the flower shop."
Says, Gomez.
Redhead Girl, refocusing:
"When do we get those bastards? We must catch these felons. Even though as of now, we have no idea, who pulled the trigger."

"We are looking forward to an update from the coroner's office. This will give us more ammunition to work with. They must be heading west to Monaco if they stick to their itinerary. Abandoning their former means of transportation indicates they could have resorted to the rail out of Gare De Nice Ville SCNF. However, these two facial looks could have resembled the man for whom we are hunting."
Billy Black removes the two wigs from a sack.
Vince Taylor is thrilled to learn these details and responds:
"Really? So, the man we are looking for is not who he is according to those looks? This is so uncanny."
Other Pips are startled. Redhead Girl leans into the huddle wanting more. However, The Pips leave her an open floor.
Redhead Girl corroborates,
"That is him! Yes! That is him in those pictures."
"This is another bad move on his part; inefficiently covering his tracks."
Says, Billy Black.
Ralph Gomez chimes in,
"I wished we had more clues."
Billy Black saving face,
"If I arrived at that abandoned car ten minutes later, this entire investigation could have gone up in smoke, fire, and debris. Turning this organized search into a sham. There is no shame in our game!"

"Ridiculous! We could have been attending your wake..."
Says, Madison Allen.
Yovanda Nichols interrupts,
"And singing Kumbaya... Timing is everything."
Billy Black submerges the sentiment and shares the pair of train tickets with his group. They pore over.
"Any other questions before we depart for the train? That train departs in an hour, according to the tickets. Unless they like his hairstyle is fake."
Madison Allen eying her iPad's screen,
"On the other hand, if those tickets are valid: according to SNCF that train is on schedule. What is our plan of attack? According to the pictures, this man has no social media presence. Not even IG or a once-used Facebook page. Her IG page has been on hiatus for almost weeks."
"He is ours. Let us work out our plan of attack but leave room for our intuition to massage the game plan."
Says, Billy Black.
"What are the real features that currently describe these two banditos? What do we have to go on? Now that they are in the hairstyling business."
States, Al Nobles.
Yovanda Nichols chuckles, and states:
"Experts in disguise? As far as we know he could be looking like every other Frenchman, crafty and

cunning. And her? A sophisticated French Lady, Mademoiselle. Like him, maybe she looks aged somewhat, with minor wrinkles? What does her mother look like? His dad? Answers could be buried in their past."

Redhead Girl raises her hand,

"That might be a clue. As far as we know: He's Caucasian and on the run. That is what we must go on. Every Caucasian man could now become a suspect, right? How do we unmask and take him out? I mean take him down before he knocks over another bank."

Redhead Girl smiles at her brilliance.

"We will have to people-watch.

Sunglasses are on the Department. Once Aziz is spotted, we will order the train to stop in the middle of nowhere. Crossing those electrical tracks can be fatal. They would not dare pull that off even if they were still collaborating. I say that because no one knows if they are still on this run together or not. That remains the unanswered question."

Says, Billy Black.

"If they try to escape, we will watch them fry."

Says, Ralph Gomez.

"So, at this point, we will move through the train cars and take them down.

Says, Redhead Girl.

She is center stage.

"A huge percentage of that train route through Monaco is hilly, treacherous, and overlooks the shoreline."

The focus is shifted to Yovanda Nichols, eager to speak:

"Yep. At this point, they are out of options and must surrender. We do not need any mishaps, we will avoid all residential neighborhoods, just a clean surrender. We will have to rely mostly on their body language. A criminal cannot avoid showing signs of guilt. Their swagger gives them up."

Billy Black reaches for his jacket and slides it on:

"I cannot believe in these modern times our Man does not even have an IG page. Yep. That is the game plan, play-by-play. All options available to us must be implemented."

Madison Allen asks,

"What if they attempt to flee the train?"

"If none of these clues permeate, we will still have to catch them. Remember, focus on the King Moves!"

Says, Billy Black.

The meeting adjourns with each one challenged.

CHAPTER NINE

The Gare De Nice Ville Train platform is crowded. The bullet train SQUEALS to a complete stop.
The Pips wearing sunglasses hustle toward the platform. They scan everyone in sight as the Passengers de-train and board. Aziz Michael and Crystal Banks are not among the passengers.
The train conductors orchestrate a nonverbal countdown.

Vince Taylor with his long lens camera, boards in car #2.

Al Nobles with his miniature binoculars, capturing everything he sees, boards in car #3.

Yovanda Nichols with her braids blowing in the wind, boards in car #4.

She totes a small, wheeled weekender, binoculars strapped around her neck. Her additional diving gear peeps out from the other bag on her shoulder.

Corrie Phelps follows with her bouquet in one hand and tennis racquets in the next. She boards in car #5.

Madison Allen tails Phelps. Madison, as always very protective of her iPad, and sunglasses, boards in car #6.

Ralph Gomez boards in car #7, toting his make-up accessories.

Passengers continue to de-train and board this bullet train. The train departs from the station.

Billy Black, aboard car #1 surveys every passenger. His phone chirps. He attends.

Peer in on the new message. Madison Allen: Mr. Black, I'll update you in a few. Hang tight. My source is talking!

Madison Allen personalizes her iPad and seeks semi-privacy on the crowded train car.

She texts: According to the Airline's flight manifest, our man's name is Aziz Michael, and his accomplice Crystal Banks, a model whom he kidnapped in

Dubai. According to my sources the two boarded in Abu Dhabi. No idea why their identities were suppressed for so long.

On her iPad, Billy Black responds: Anything else? Motive? Who claimed responsibility?

Madison Allen responds: That is all for now. Still working on my sources. I will keep you posted.

Billy Black responds: Thanks. We'll arrive in Monaco in fifteen minutes. Stay on it! Press them!

The train moves along rapidly towards Monaco.

CHAPTER TEN

The PIPS, arrive at the Monaco Train Station, challenged. They disembark, riveted. They survey. There is no sign of Crystal Banks and Aziz Michael. At the Monaco Station, Billy Black meets with an Informer, Chris Isaacs. Chris hands over a thumb drive to him.

Moments later:

The Pips huddle at a nearby parking lot. Billy Black hands the thumb drive to Madison Allen. She inserts it into her iPad. They huddle. The FOOTAGE ROLLS:

The train bound from Nice pulls into the Monaco Station. Passengers embark and disembark.

The at large Aziz Michael wearing a baseball cap and Crystal Banks wearing a multi-colored head-tie amongst the detraining passengers.

They hustle for a waiting Taxi. Each one toting a small, wheeled weekender piece of luggage.

Aziz and Banks board a waiting Taxi. The Taxi motors off.

FOOTAGE ENDS

THE PARKING LOT thins out.

Billy Black seems disillusioned. He shakes his head under the strain of the shifted momentum.

"They are one step ahead of us. We will leave no stone unturned until we find them."

"What if they are headed to Italy?"

Asks, Redhead Girl.

Billy Black rallies his team:

"It doesn't matter. We will hunt them down in the caves of Afghanistan if necessary. We're in this for the long haul."

Redhead Girl asks,

"How long do you think they will keep on running?

Billy Black responds,
"Until they get tired, or we catch up with them. Whichever comes first. "Meanwhile, Ralph Gomez rallies his teammates,
"I like the latter scenario. If they do not know who is on their trail... They are about to find out..."
Even so, The Pips eye the hills of Monaco with mixed emotions.

CHAPTER ELEVEN

Vince Taylor is still glued to the Hills of Monaco,
"Those hills are not as treacherous as they seem."
Yovanda Nichols semi-glued to the hills,
"For you, they aren't as bad. Navigating on the water would add to our defense; just in case they opt for a Mediterranean getaway."
She would rather hunt on water, and not in those treacherous hills of Monaco.

Billy Black focuses on the chase on hand:
"Let's divide up to conquer. Hills or no hills. Nichols, the ship is at the dock ready to go if necessary."
Redhead Girl buoyed:
"I like what I am hearing. Slice and dice! Bring them to their knees. Hitting them where it hurts is to our advantage in this manhunt.
Madison Allen, eying the strapped Corrie Phelps:
"You are a quick study, aren't you? Have you fired one of those?
Redhead Girl responds,
"It is said: What one does in practice, can be done in sleep or when severely challenged in a wink."
Billy Black looks at Madison Allen and assesses.
"Madison Allen, find a lookout venue and do what you do best.
He looks at Ralph Gomez,
"Gomez, I need you to frequent the French Cuisine."
He looks at Redhead Girl,
"Phelps, scout the streets looking at anything tennis related."
He looks across at Al Nobles,
"Nobles, window shop on Monte Carlo."
He looks at Vince Taylor,
"Vince Taylor, you are a tourist, ask suspects for locations."
Redhead Giri is openmouthed,
That's all? What about me?

Billy Black:

"Additionally, Hit up the train, taxi, and bus stations.

I'll have the hills of Monaco. Let's get to work on this manhunt."

CHAPTER TWELVE

Subsequently, a van pulls up. Its sign reads Monte Carlo Rentals. The Pips prepare to board. Suddenly, a black Mercedes Benz pulls up. Billy Black, yet to board, tarries with his camera in hand.
The two Frenchmen, in cahoots at the Gas Station, Motorist #3 and Motorist #4, dressed in business attire create a standoff. Both men are still strangers

to the eyes of Billy Black. They jump out showing off cameras like Billy Black's.

Motorist # 3, greets:

"Nice camera. I love Cannons. I own at least half a dozen of them. The one you are holding is my fav, mirrorless."

Billy Black responds:

"Is this the How to Win Friends and Influence People session?"

"Not really!"

Responds, Motorist #3.

Onboard van: Tension mounts among the PIPS. They are fixated on the two Frenchmen engaging Billy Black. Yovanda Nichols draws her gun and aims at the men. The others follow suit.

The conversation continues between Billy Black and the two men amid high stakes.

Motorist #4 displays a sign:

"Have you seen these two?"

The men are resilient.

Billy Black remains poised, caressing his weapon:

"Aziz Michael and Crystal Banks. How much?"

Motorist #4 eying Banks' weapon:

"Twenty Thousand Euros!"

Billy Black asks:

"Cash? Who pays?"

Motorist #3 responds,

"Yep. We are well-sourced. Half up front and the other half after delivery at your designated drop box."
Motorist #4 hands Billy Black his business card.
MOTORIST #4 states,
"Call me. This is an offer you can't pass up, Black."
Billy Black countering,
"What is their significance to your covert operation?"
Motorist #4 defends,
"Covert? Don't get hung up with the tea leaves. That's classified. Call me if you are up to the task. If not, we'll find someone else who wants to conduct our demands."
Billy Black responds,
"You fail to realize that we are irreplaceable."
Billy Black turns away towards the van. He boards the waiting van, challenged.
There is SILENCE.
Yovanda Nichols zeroes in on the men's departure. She returns the gun to its holster.
Yovanda Nichols focuses on Billy Black,
"What was that all about, quid pro quo?"
"Looks like we have competition at an elevated level with a big, fat, dangling purse."
States, Billy Black.
"Really?"
Yovanda Nichols asks.

"As far as I could tell. They are after the Nice Killers too."

Says, Billy Black.

Yovanda Nichols says to Billy Black:

"I have seen those two cats before. Frick and Frack. They were on a white luxury yacht that pulled into Cannes yesterday. Not only were their cameras regularly active. They invited me on board."

Eyes peel at Yovanda Nichols, more so, The Redhead Girl.

Yovanda Nichols responds naively and shares her cell phone pictures of the two men with the Pips team. Eyes widen, staring at Yovanda Nichols, who states:

"I sense something sinister about those two dudes. Now they are stepping up their conspiracy."

CHAPTER THIRTEEN

Yovanda Nichols recounts mentally the experience. The Pips visually enter that space with her:
Yovanda Nichols swimming in her bikini at Cannes beach. Multiple luxury yachts are docked in the bay nearby.
Yovanda sees another luxury yacht sail by. Two men aboard wearing sailor hats are stuck on her

sensuality. They wave at her, beckoning her to their designated dock. She declines.
They persist.
Yovanda Nichols straps herself, pulls a bathrobe over her weapon, grabs her binoculars, and complies.
Arriving at their dock.
Motorist #3 & Motorist #4 greet her from the deck:
Bonjour Madame!
Yovanda Nichols responds:
Bonjour Sailors.
Motorist #4 replies:
Miss Nigeria, would you mind joining us for a sail around Cannes or sit back and chat casually while we're here in port for dinner or drinks?
Yovanda Nichols asks:
Where are you from?
Motorist #3 replies,
Paradise.
Yovanda Nichols asks:
Really?
Motorist #3 replies,
Yep.
Yovanda Nichols states:
You are mooring at a very crowded bay. Necessity?
Motorist #3 responds:
We love it here in Cannes. This is our Jamaica.
Yovanda Nichols asks:

Really? I do not make it a habit of accepting invites on my swim day. But I can't oblige. Time is of the essence, though.

Motorist #3 states:

Step aboard! We will honor your wishes. All work and no play make Jill a dull girl.

Yovanda Nichols states,

And Jack the stood upper, yep?

They chuckle. She joins them at a table on deck.

Motorist #4 asks:

Champagne? What's your preference?

Yovanda Nichols says,

Crystal.

Motorist #4 says,

We are out. Do you care for Mowhet?

Yovanda Nichols responds,

I am a Crystal woman and would not settle...

Motorist #3 replies,

We can get you whatever your appetite desires and have it delivered promptly.

Motorist #4 gets on his phone, attempting to score with her.

Hi. This is Franco. Can you drop off a case of Crystal at the Whisky? Thanks.

Yovanda looks both men over and senses something sinister amid them falling all over themselves to accommodate her.

Gentlemen, you are killing the foreplay.

She reaches for her cell phone.
Yovanda Nichols into the phone:
"I will be there soon. Bye.
(to the two men)
I have an emergency. Plus, you do not have what my taste buds desire. Timing is everything. Try better planning on your part next time. At least have Crystal if you are inviting me up for drinks.:"
She leaves speedily.

CHAPTER FOURTEEN

Returning to the present. Billy Black ponders after browsing the pics on Yovanda Nichol's iPhone.
"Yep. That is them. Same swagger."
Eyeing the biz card.
"Hmmm. An interesting twist of events, Al Franco. I smell machination against us."
Yovanda nods,
"Yes."

"In life, you either play big or go home. They are playing for a flush."

Says, Billy Black.

"Could they be operating from the inside? Is Welch in on this?"

Asks, Yovanda Nichols.

Billy Black answers,

"Possibly. The cream always rises to the top. Too much heat in the kitchen for him."

Up ahead. The Monte Carlo Rentals sign looms. While their advancement hastens.

"I am not going home. Who is up to taking me on in tennis, afterward?"

Redhead Girl challenges.

Ralph looks across at Yovanda Nichols and chuckles. Ralph Gomez chimes in,

"I thought you were related to Serena Williams."

Yovanda Nichols watching the tennis champ at the recent US Open on her cellphone,

"Darn. I wished. I sure could spend her money."

Madison Allen, challenged by Phelps invite,

"Corrie, I am not a Serena Williams, but I am up for the challenge after the hunt. Are you game?"

"Sounds like a plan. Service! Service! Serve!"

Yells, Corie Phelps.

Chuckles reverberate among the group regarding Corrie's jest.

Moments later: They arrive at Monte Carlo Car Rentals.

The Pips transfer to, and head out in separate vehicles forming a convoy. A long bridge beckons. Their eclectic vehicles swiftly merge thereon.

Obliviously to the Pips: Motorists #3 and #4 capture departing shots of their convoy speeding away.

CHAPTER FIFTEEN

Madison Allen is riveted at a lookout, logging information into her iPad. She captures images to support the already-gathered evidence on the manhunt. Yet, no one who fits the likes of Aziz Michael and Crystal Banks arises.

Noticeable though The Pips remain resilient. Ralph Gomez is seen dining at the French Cuisine.

Redhead Girl is incognito outside a sporting goods store. She windows shops.

The shopping traffic remains heavy. Masses of Gen Z shoppers and grown-ups are mobile, but Madison Allen realizes no one matches nobody on her target list- no Aziz or Crystal.

In the interim, Al Nobles window shops in Monte Carlo. Like an advertising bag man, he is laden with shopping bags. He sees a pony-tailed subject trolling on the sidewalk. He trails momentarily but soon validates that man as an Aziz Michael mistaken identity.

Vince Taylor wearing a straw hat hits up train, taxi, and bus stations. Vince sees and woman boarding a train. He boards behind them. He investigates. They are looking at him. He is looking at them.

They do not match the looks of Aziz Michael and Crystal Banks. How he wished they did.

The train waits in the station with doors open. Vince Taylor apologetically smiles at the couple and de-trains.

While Yovanda Nichols is seen traversing the Monaco Dock. She is fixated on a Couple on board a sailing yacht, and even boards a dinghy and in an investigative mood sails towards the yacht.

Disappointingly, she realizes they are not Aziz and Crystal.

Meanwhile, Billy Black is seen in a car navigating the hills of Monaco. He sees a husband and wife, jogging. He stops his auto and gets their attention. They stop their jogging in response.

Billy Black states,

"I am Billy Black with the Pips. Looking for the shooters."

He shows them the pictures on his phone of Aziz and Crystal.

The Husband responds,

"Sorry, I have not seen them."

His Wife leaning in,

"They were at U Seven... In the grocery aisle. They later took off in a bright red-orange automobile."

Billy Black asks,

"Did you see their license tags?"

Husband whispers in his Wife's ear

"Tell him we must go.

My wife plays in the team,

"Sorry, I do not work for the police"

Billy Black hands them an olive branch.

"Thanks for your help."

Billy Black returns to his auto. It motors off.

CHAPTER SIXTEEN

Lovemaking sounds emit from this exclusive Monaco mountainous wooden hideaway.
Moments later: Aziz Michael and Crystal Banks walk onto the balcony. His left-hand gropes around her waist.
She turns into him and vice versa. They kiss passionately. He wants more, and she reluctantly complies.

Finally, they release each other and find themselves staring at the hills bordering the domain.

The panoramic view of the ocean pops. It grabs their attention, tightly. Her eyes glitter. He and her seem coupled, although briefly.

Suddenly, she ponders and tears up. He strokes her neck. She sighs and dries her tears.

His hand slides down her lower back. She is tickled. She forcibly chuckles. He laughs heartily.

She is nostalgic and releases herself hastily from his grasp.

CRYSTAL BANKS calculatingly asks,

"When are you going to take me back?

Why are you trying to destroy me? This was not the way this was supposed to go down. I was promised a modeling job - all business."

AZIZ MICHAEL responds,

"I thought by now that question was a foregone conclusion."

Crystal Banks asks,

"Answered? By whom? You are still imagining things, Aziz. This relationship is fabricated. It is manufactured. Can't you tell, there is nothing between us... forcing one against their will? Who are you? A murderer!"

"I could be characterized as burying my victims before they are dead. You did say you would rather be with me than anyone else, didn't you?"

Asks, Aziz.

Crystal Banks digs in,

"There you go again. You never heard those words from me. There was no reason for that Teller to be shot."

Aziz reaches for her hands and caresses her fingers. He seizes her hand and leads her back inside. Crystal stiffens up.

After an interval.

They return to the deck. Crystal holding a glass of champagne and vice versa. They toast, cheer forcibly, and sip on the Mowhet champagne.

Crystal seems more troubled, nursing a half-full glass of champagne.

Aziz Michael drills down,

"After all, I've done to pry you away from Dough. Furthermore, he has seldom treated you kindly. Don't you get it? Remember, you told me that night he punched you so hard, that you were hospitalized for over a week. There shouldn't be any reason to be so frigid towards me. You are as cold as ice. Even the birds in the trees, and the crickets... celebrate their warmth."

CRICKETS CHIRP

BIRDS SING

Aziz Michael continues,

"How the crickets cherish our togetherness."

Crystal Banks replies,

"That still doesn't justify your actions. If I could only be where I belong, that would make all the difference in the world to me."

"I thought you were starved for hearing the birds sing, the crickets chirp, and the frog croak. Plus, the waves washing up against the shore, and watching the branches of the trees sway and swagger?"

Says, Aziz Michael.

Aziz stares deep into her eyes, her soul, and then at his half-empty glass of Champagne and Crystal's, still half full. He is guilt-stricken, and beyond as he tries a double take.

Crystal Banks mirrors:

"If only I could conceal this ambiance in a bottle and take it away with me, to someplace where I can let my guard down, and not be hypnotized. A place where I am not held hostage."

Aziz Michael is challenged:

"So, what's wrong with this place?"

Crystal Banks holding her own,

"Home is where the heart is... void of witnessing five bullets penetrate one's skull. Why? For money? Money comes, money goes. No one has ever been mummified with currencies... "

His cell phone rings. He saunters inside to get it.

Crystal follows but changes her mind, detours, and returns to the deck half-robed, revealing her curves, accentuated by her sexy underwear. She profiles entertaining a catwalk-viewing audience.

The patio furniture, beckons. Crystal answers and lies face down on the chair. Her sensuality pops, especially from her curvaceous backside. She knows she is hot.

A Male Guest from the hotel across the adjacent hill, waves at her. She ignores the greeting. The guest persists. She disregards his overtures.

Oblivious to her, Motorists #3 and #4 are stationed on the upper floor of that hotel, which houses the Male Guest. They are camera-ready, and covertly capturing footage of Crystal's latest appearance.

CHAPTER SEVENTEEN

Motorists #3 and #4 put their cameras away and enjoy a shared scenic ride down the scenic hills. Motorist #3 drives his Mercedes Benz with Motorist #4 - the passenger in the front seat. Like Bud and Lou, they are comically rattled.
The CAR PHONE RINGS
Motorist #3 answers in speaker mode.
It is Investigator Welch.

INTERCUTTING between Investigator Welch at his offices, and Motorist # 3 and #4 in the BMW driving down the mountain.

Welch greets,

"Hey, Franco, you have been MIA."

"No. Talk to me. Dobbs is here with me. We are enjoying some scenic views in these hills while staying mission driven."

Motorist # 3 answers.

Investigator Welch asks,

"Are you mission-driven, Dobbs?"

Motorist #4 answers,

"Yes, Sir. We need to move this case forward. Way too many tea leaves..."

Investigator Welch asks,

"Did Billy Black buy into the offer?"

Motorist #4 responds,

"He's like a woman; playing hard to get. He's still sitting on my phone number and email address."

Motorist #3 states,

"The clock is ticking. We've got to get Aziz alive before they take him out dead. That is still the goal, right?"

Investigator Welch says,

"Yep. If he hasn't called you back, that could be a signal they want Aziz Michael and Crystal Banks dead not alive. At their department, Billy Black is in charge."

Motorist #4 says,

"Should we call him and up the price? He might bite, now."

Investigator Welch responds,

"I would say double the value. By now everyone and their momma could be in on the catch, even Dubai wants in on the capture."

Motorist #4 responds,

"Got it! Welch, now this is all adding up. We'll get back to you."

Investigator Welch states,

"Time is running out, guys!"

CHAPTER EIGHTEEN

In the United Arab Emirates, in a regional trading hub known as Dubai, a Limo pulls up in a chic Villa. Crystal Banks' husband, DOUG BANKS in his 40s, walks out to the vehicle.
Two centralized Arab Indian Men step out and greet. Doug Banks is focused.
"Finish the job!"
He says.
The men nod "Yes" and re-board the limo.

Douglas Banks returns to the Villa, queried.

Back in Monaco, Motorist #3 dials Billy Black. He reaches the VOICEMAIL.

We are Pips, your Private Investigation Protective Service. If you have information that could lead to the arrest of Aziz Michael and Crystal Banks, please let us know. All communications will be kept confidential. Thanks for your assistance in bringing criminals to justice.

Motorist #3 aborts the call.

Motorist #4 states:

"He's still on the case. Yet, he refuses to talk with us. This could be his payday."

Motorist #3 suggests,

"Why didn't you leave him a message and a callback number?"

"It's always a good thing to maintain some posture. Black has my contacts. He'll call before this is over."

Replies, Motorist #4.

The two Indian Men arrive in Monaco, assessed. They peruse the enclaves without any glance at Crystal Banks or their target Aziz Michael.

CHAPTER NINETEEN

Later, Aziz and Crystal dine at an exclusive Monaco restaurant. He's upbeat, but she's not in good spirits. The bottle of red wine on the table is almost consumed. The agile, attentive Waitress ambles across and serves from another bottle. Aziz and Crystal cheer, and they indulge.

Aziz Michael looks intensely into Crystal's eyes. "What are you thinking?"

Crystal Banks replies,

"God gives life, and man in a desire to outwit God, takes it away. Malcolm Yates' death terrifies me."

Aziz Michael gets up to leave the table.

"Excuse me. I'll be right back."

He moseys towards the restroom. Time passes. He doesn't return. Seemingly restless, Crystal surveys the restaurant. She consumes the bottle of red wine and grabs a cigarette and lighter from her purse. Clutches the purse and strolls outside.

Crystal displays confidence lights up a cigarette and takes multiple swift tokes while gazing at the stars.

A masked man comes up to her, mask-tapes her mouth, blindfolds her, and escorts her inside a getaway car. The car motors off speedily.

Patrons and Restaurant employees noticing elements of the abduction, rush outside. Too late. The getaway car has vanished.

Aziz returns to the table. He finds Crystal missing. Showing no contrition, he heads outside carrying the vase of flowers once sitting on the dining table.

Aziz elevates himself, removes the flowers, and crushes the bouquet under his feet. He gets inside the car. It motors off in the same direction as the getaway vehicle transporting Crystal.

CHAPTER TWENTY

Monaco is in a frenzy. Emergency sounds envelope.
SIRENS CRESCENDO
DRONES SURVEY
EMERGENCY VEHICLES ROLL
RESCUE HELICOPTERS TAKE TO THE SKIES
A picture-taking pilot in a helicopter joins the search. Other Helicopters surveil Monaco and high-density areas. On the ground, French Police with dogs, comb

through the neighborhoods. There is no sight of Crystal or Aziz.

The Pips join the search without a trace.

The sun rises and shines through the trees in the woods, providing clarity. Police comb through the woods with dogs. Yet, there is no rescue recovery.

Hours later. Suddenly, someone is spotted in the woods. It is a female with long hair.

Could this be Crystal Banks?

Rescuers travel deep into the woods to rescue that subject. News surfaces in the local paper that Crystal Banks was allegedly seen in the woods walking alone.

The Dubai News is reporting that Super Model Crystal Banks who has been missing for more than a week, possibly kidnapped, and feared dead could still be alive and residing in France.

Several rescuers cool their heels thereafter.

French Police rescuers searching in the woods, come up on the young adult.

Investigator Welch, heading up the search is confused. Close up. The image does not look like Crystal Banks.

"Miss, what is your name? We need to see an ID."

She reaches inside her purse and presents a picture ID. Investigator Welch looks it over.

Investigator Welch states:

"MADELINE JACKSON? Miss, you are not who we are looking for. But what are you doing deep in these woods? Don't you realize that you are putting yourself in harm's way? Are you Madeline Jackson?"
Madeline goes mute.
Other Investigators join the huddle.
Investigator Welch asks,
"Are you able to speak?"
Madeline Jackson, trembling from the cold says under her breath:
"Madeline Jackson!"
Investigator Welch asks,
Madeline, once again I must ask,
"Why are you in these woods?"
SILENCE
She begins to shiver.
"Possible foul play? TBD"
States Investigator Welch.
Two rescuers emerge. They place Madeline on a stretcher and escort her out of the woods.

CHAPTER TWENTY-ONE

Two masked men show up outside Billy Black's home. The light is on in the living room. One rings the doorbell. No one answers.

They scan the block to identify Billy Black's vehicle and slash all four tires. Black's auto is left sitting on its rims and keyed - GET OUT OF TOWN.

Over at Investigator Welch's house, he is sitting in his living room. The TV is on. He is sipping on his fav "Kro"1664 beer.

His cell phone rings. He answers, briskly.
It is Motorist #4.
"Welch, we've searched hard for Billy Black. Still nothing. Anyway..."
Investigator Welch asks,
"Anyway, what? I got it! Take care of business. Time is running out. We cannot let Billy Black control this narrative. My guys would have already completed the job."
Motorist #4 responds:
"We've heard in the news that you found a woman alive in the woods. Was that really Crystal Banks?"
Investigator Welch states:
"You are late on this one. A case of mistaken identity. This means that you and Dobbs must bring the "A" game before Billy Black gets to them. He'll show no mercy."
Motorist #3 responds,
"Billy Black is going to have much catching up to make that happen, sir."
In the interim, Billy Black dressed in a jogging suit, returns home. He notices his Auto sitting on its four rims. He enters the house and hits Playback on his Home Security Device. It reveals Motorist #3 and #4 in the act - vandalizing his automobile. He's irate as to who must have done it.

CHAPTER TWENTY-TWO

At The Pips Headquarters, Vince Taylor sits at his desk. He looks exhausted. Footage rolls. The News interrupts his chore.

"The quest in the search for Crystal Banks turns up in a mistaken identity... According to sources, the image of the woman spotted yesterday in the woods of Southern France turned out to be that of a young adult woman, Madeline Jackson. Not much has been

said about why the woman was roaming in the woods. More to come on this unfolding story."
Reports, the NEWS ANCHOR.
Vince Taylor counters,
"Why in the name of God does she choose to remain silent regarding a matter so palpable to investigators? Who is she protecting?"
Vince Taylor closes the attaché, peeved, and powers up a laptop. It is a busy day at the office. Pips Investigators traverse.
Vince Taylor is glued to his computer, with Billy Black standing over him while he is researching Madeline Jackson. He lands on her IG Page.
Vince Taylor states,
"Not much to find except an IG page with pics of Madeline Jackson, associated with multiple feminist organizations."
The landline phone in the office rings. Billy Black answers:
"Tell her to come inside."
Madeline Jackson walks in amidst Vince Taylor's perusal. Vince conceals the computer search upon her arrival.
Billy Black welcomes:
"Miss Jackson thanks for coming down. We admire your bravery and commitment to justice and value this opportunity to speak with you."

Other Pips arrive and huddle around Madeline to catch every word.

CHAPTER TWENTY-THREE

Billy Black focuses on his team. Madeline seems very apprehensive. Billy Black asks:
"Does anyone have any questions for Miss Jackson?"
The initiative-taking Redhead Girl asks,
"Miss Jackson, I am Corrie Phelps. Why were you really in those woods, alone?"
Madeline Jackson pulls herself together and responds,
"I was looking for that woman."

Redhead Girl asks,
"Crystal Banks?"
"Yes, Crystal."
Redhead Girl asks,
"Weren't you afraid you were putting yourself in harm's way and could get killed?"
Madeline Jackson responds,
"All my life I have desired to become a female activist."
She tears up but continues:
"If a man has not discovered something he would die for, he is not fit to live. Those were the words of the late Dr. Martin Luther King Jr, yes? Sometimes someone must die for someone else to live."
Al Nobles paces,
"Yep! I have heard enough. I am going into those woods."
Billy Black asks,
"Now?"
Al Nobles states,
"Tomorrow, at daybreak."
"By yourself, Al? Aren't you going to need backup?"
Asks, Ralph Gomez.
Al is stone-faced.
"Al, it has been three days. Do you think she could still be alive?"
Asks Nichols.

"It is possible. There comes a time when a man must decide which cause is of utmost importance to him. I have got this!"
Says, Al Nobles.
Madison Allen teaming up:
"There is a state-of-the-art GPS on my iPad."
"Al Nobles, I've got your back."
Says Billy Black.
"Amen!"
Says Madeline Jackson.
All heads turn towards Al Nobles and Madeline Jackson in appreciation.

CHAPTER TWENTY-FOUR

A ray of light penetrates through the fog in the woods. Al Nobles, dressed in army fatigues swings a flashlight in search. Suddenly, he stops in his tracks. Then proceeds rapidly toward an object.
He notices it's a blood-drenched corpse in his path. Al maintains a rapid but cautious pace. Covering his nose, he moves towards the remains. He steps back and radios.

" I have found her!"
Says Al Nobles.
"How do you know it is her... Al?
　　　　Asks, Billy Black.
"Her passport was discovered at the crime scene. Plus, the corpse is a replica of the picture the Man gave to you in Nice."
Says, Al Nobles.
"Okay. Hawkish on all evidence... One part is over, the other has just begun. We are coming in!"
Says, Billy Black.
Back at Pips Headquarters, the Pips team departs in a van. The radio plays low, soft pop music. Suddenly, the music fades.
The NEWS intercepts.
The death of Crystal Banks hit her hometown this morning when the airwaves announced her death. According to sources, her body was found in the woods of France near Monaco. Crystal was abducted in Dubai more than a week ago and brought to France. Her alleged abductor, Aziz Michael, is said to still be at large. Numerous Dubai models have reined in since her disappearance. More on this story at the top of the hour.
Other Pips peripherally focus their attention on Billy Black for the next move.
"I sense we are nearing a resolution in this case."
Says Redhead Girl.

"You are right. We are staying on this case until Aziz Michael is hunted down. That is our mission."
Says Billy Black.
Redhead Girl shouts:
"Mission accomplished!"

CHAPTER TWENTY-FIVE

The van pulls up at the crime scene. They jump out. Al Nobles, greets. The crime scene is grotesque. Although distorted, and butchered, the features are those of the model - Crystal Banks.
A team of Investigators along with Pathologists from multiple law enforcement agencies swarmed onto the scene. They collect evidence, supervised by

Investigator Welch on one side, and Billy Black with his Pips floating.

Welch gives Billy Black an approval nod. Billy Black smiles back, modestly.

A preponderance of evidence discovered at the crime scene includes (a)The mutilated body of Crystal Banks. (b)Man's wallet, later identified to belong to Aziz Michael. (c)The vase previously seen at the restaurant was filled with flowers and broken into multiple shares. (d) Crystal Bank's passport.

Later that day. The Pips return to Base Camp.

At the supraorbital torus of the meeting room, hitched is a large TV monitor. We see the footage collected from Informer, Chris Isaacs running repeatedly MOS.

Al Nobles opens up the discussion.

"If I were authoring this story as a crime novel, I would say Aziz is a very twisted character to contend with."

"I am with you on that, Al"

Says, Billy Black.

"Why did he choose France as his escape route?"

Asks, Al Nobles.

"He thought he would catch us napping, asleep at the wheel."

Responds, Billy Black.

"If he is not the one who murdered Crystal Banks. Why was his wallet discovered at the crime scene?

Her passport? She must have been planning a getaway to Dubai."

States, Redhead Girl.

Did she take off with his wallet, and he had to struggle with her to retrieve it? This is very uncharacteristic. Was it left there intentionally?

Yovanda Nichols asks,

"How is he going to prove that he was not there?"

Billy Black responds,

"He forgot the three-letter word."

"I have my iPad open. What is that three-letter word?"

Asks, Madison Allen.

We all have it. It defines who we are, and where we have been.

States, Billy Black.

Al Nobles seems to have it nailed,

"Yep. His DNA was all over that crime scene. It was fresh! Did he or did he not kill Crystal Banks?"

"Al Nobles, you win again. All indications point to his presence at the crime scene. He got her the flowers, then he crushed those flowers and allegedly used the vase to help butcher her. Remember those mangled flowers found outside that restaurant where they dined together?"

States, Redhead Girl.

"We will not find out until we catch him alive. Let us hit the streets!"

Says Billy Black.

His phone rings. He signals, "Private." The rest of the Pips head out as he facilitates the call.

CHAPTER TWENTY-SIX

Billy Black answers his phone.
"This is Billy Black!"
INTERCUTING between Billy Black on the phone, and SMOOTH JOE, who speaks like a Con Man. He is a Frenchman and a wanna-be cop. Smooth Joe, paces with one hand inside his hip pocket as if he is armed.
"Billy Black, this is Smooth Joe."

"Smooth Joe, I know. Your timing is impeccable. Heading to Cannes. Will be there in less than an hour."
Says, Billy Black.
Smooth Joe responds,
"Meet me at Le Majestic Lounge.
Yovanda Nichols, in high eavesdropping mode, approaches:
"Putting out another fire?"
"Yep. At Le Majestic!"
Billy Black responds.
Yovanda Nichols asks,
"Taking us along for the chase?"
Billy Blak responds,
"Keep an eye on Nice. I will keep you posted."
"Really?"
Asks, Nichols.
"Meeting someone new is always stepping out on faith."
Billy Black responds.
Yovanda looks across at the rest of the Pips, huddled.
"Is this the way you are choosing to make your exit, faith?"
Asks Nichols.
Billy Black responds,
"Whenever you board a commercial airline. You do not enter the cockpit and check to see who is or if

anyone is flying the darn thing. You just find your seat, fasten your seat belt, and anticipate you'll get to your destination."

Al Nobles interjects:

"He is right Nichols. That is in his DNA. The man must do what he has to do. Sometimes alone."

Yovanda Nichols rolled her eyes,

"In a sense, I am being overly protective."

Says, Billy Black throws on his trench coat and heads out.

Later. Billy Black pulls into the driveway at Le Majestic. Numerous Ad signs add decor.

A valet steps up.

Billy Black hands over his automobile keys and steps through the hotel door to a semi-crowded lobby.

A Concierge meet and greet.

Billy Black states,

"Here to see Smooth Joe?"

The Concierge points to the longue.

CHAPTER TWENTY-SEVEN

Seated at a semi-private table, Smooth Joe is smoking a cigar. A half-full beer bottle sits on the table. Billy Black pulls up a chair.
"Joe., you wanted to meet with me. What have you got?"
Asks, Billy Black.
Smooth Joe asks,
"Drink?"

Billy Black sizes him up. Measuring the situation.
"Thanks, but no thanks. Not with a gun in its holster and meeting with a stranger."
Smooth Joe responds,
"Billy Black, you should know that the smell of Sulphur does not scare me."
Smooth Joe lifts his shirt.
Billy Black, on the defense, draws his weapon.
"Don't be so trigger-happy. I am just showing you my scars."
Smooth Joe reveals multiple bullet scars on his stomach.
Billy Black returning his weapon,
"Wow! Me, neither. "
Billy Black does vice vera, revealing bullet scars across the breadth of his stomach, exhibiting the armed shoulder holster.
Billy Black continues,
"That is why I am always armed."
PAUSE.
"There are only 24 hours in a day. What have you got?"
Asks Billy Black.
A sexy Waitress serves Smooth Joe another beer. Joe stares her down. Server locks eyes with Billy Black, her pen poised to write.
Billy Black states,
"Police business. I will pass."

The server departs with uneasiness in her eyes.
Smooth Joe gets down to business,
"Black, I have not heard back from your HR Department, let them know I'm still up for the gig if they are ready to move on me. At least I could be the chauffeur for the Pips squad, pick up your clothes from the cleaners, etc."
Billy Black, not feeling him would rather talk about leads to Aziz. Smooth Joe clues in.
"Anyway, your Man Aziz Michael, who you're hunting, was seen on the docks at Cannes last night."
Really? By whom? Any footage?
Asks Billy Black.
"You know he is from Dubai and goes in style. Man's a Baller. He had to come through here and spend a wad of that oil money he drilled from Nigeria."
Billy Black asks,
"So, what do you have, nothing else?
"Black. Seeing I am not on the team… yet. I chose not to stalk the man. That, to me, would have been considered overreach, do you think?"
Billy Black responds,
"Thanks for letting me know you favor a quid pro quo. You could have made a citizen's arrest or called in the Franchise."
Smooth Joe responds,
"The Franchise? Those boys travel mostly in groups of three armed with assault weapons. They might

mistake me for the hunted, and pop, pop... another Frenchman wasted."

"Regarding Aziz Michael, somebody must keep criminals at bay. Just call 112. Somebody will pick up the phone. Tough job, sometimes but someone must do it."

Says Billy Black.

"True."

Smooth Joe responds.

"So where did Aziz Michael go?"

Asks Billy Black.

" Did you mean after he left Le Majestic Hotel?"

Asks Smoot Joe.

"Was he incognito?"

Asks Billy Black.

"He certainly was not disguised. I recognized him instantly heading through the doors."

Says Billy Black.

"How much can I offer you to keep your eyes peeled until I return?"

Asks Billy Black.

Smooth Joe smiling,

"Now we are talking. It is all negotiable, Black."

Billy Black, fist bumps,

"I want that fish in my frying pan. I will fry him on one side. Turn him over and fry him on the other. You feel me. If you see him, holla at me, I will bait up for the catch."

"Copy! Never heard it said like that, Black."
Billy Black departs.
BACK IN DUBAI, the Indian men meet with Dough Banks. The stakes are high, and Dough is in a mournful state of mind.
The Elder Indian Man addresses:
"I pray the love of Allah enfolds you during your difficult times."
The Younger Indian Man states:
"Allah is always merciful towards people who believe in him."
Doug Banks is focused.
"Finish the job! Now! Do not return until Aziz Michael is delivered to me dead or alive."
The elder of the two men bows in honor to Doug.
They reboard the limo. It speeds away from the curb.

CHAPTER TWENTY-EIGHT

Billy Black stakes out inside his automobile across from Cannes Dock and nearby Le Majestic.
He dials Smooth Joe and gets VOICE MAIL,
This is Smooth Joe. The Ultimate Frenchman. I will get back.
Moments later, Billy Blacks' phone rings.
INTERCUTING between Billy Black in his parked automobile and Smooth Joe at Le Majestic.

"Smooth Joe. This is the PIPS. We show up where we say we will be rain, snow, hail, or storm. Please do not play with me. No integrity?"

"Black, your Man just got on a yacht heading to Monaco, so..."

"Why did you not stop him?"

"Black, I do not have a gun!"

"Understood. Get yourself a darn phone that answers my call. You missed that call, and now he is gone."

Smooth Joe responds,

"My bad."

Billy Black states,

"Rule Number One. Do as you are told. Keep your eyes peeled!"

"So, I flunked the audition process?"

Asks Smooth Joe.

"Most people dislike being an eight-ball. You did, Ultimate Frenchman. Do not B.S me. I can smell B.S. from as far away as the moon. You did not keep watch."

Billy Black grabs an incoming call.

It is Redhead Girl.

"Let us meet Aziz in Monaco Bay. He must be heading there."

Redhead Girl says,

"Copy that! Over."

CHAPTER TWENTY-NINE

The Pips converge on Monaco. Multiple yachts are moored into the harbor. The yacht in question is a no-show.
The Pips board Harbor Tender Yachts while validating other boats in the harbor. There's no sight of Aziz Michael. Billy Black waits at the dock inside his automobile.
A Drone Shot exposes:

A fast-moving Mercedes Benz. It is the same one depicted on Billy Black's Home Security System. He fires multiple rounds at the BMW and blows out all four tires. The vehicle slams into a wall, killing Motorists #3 and #4.

Later. A bright-orange-red car enters the zone.

Billy Black sees the profile of Aziz Michael driving the vehicle.

His auto is aggressively in pursuit.

Aziz's car speeds up.

The race continues onto a two-lane highway and a two-lane one-way street. The left lane bottlenecks, and protests ahead. The right lane reads: for Busses only.

The bright-orange-red car takes the Bus Lane for its getaway—an intersection beckons. The Pips van with tinted windows pulls up and waits. Aziz's car is trapped. Aziz exits the vehicle, attempting a getaway on foot. Behind him, Billy Black emerges on foot with a pointed gun. The foot race escalates.

The Pips' van moves towards Aziz. He attempts to shoot at the van and simultaneously at the ensuing Billy Black—his gun jams.

CLICK!

He looks for a getaway. There is none. He surrenders.

Billy Black puts handcuffs on Aziz.

Suddenly, another car pulls up. The two Indian Men last seen getting into the limo in Dubai jump out, with guns drawn on Billy Black, Aziz Michael, and the Pips.

The Redhead Girl pulls up in another car. Her gun points at the two men.

The Two Indian Men are distracted.

A round from Billy Black's gun dislodges one of their guns.

The man tries to get away and is tripped by Yovanda Nichols.

The other Indian Man tries to get one off. Too late. A round from The Redhead Girl's gun topples the gun out of his hand. Both Indian Men are captured.

Moments later: DUBAI NEWS Announces,

Aziz Michael has been captured in Monaco. Wanted for the murder and kidnapping of models Crystal Banks and Gisela Clarke. The Pips, a Southern France Investigative team helmed by Billy Black, after trailing Aziz for weeks conducted the arrest. Aziz Michael will be flown back to Dubai tomorrow where he will await trial. Two Indian men believed to have a Dubai connection were also captured and detained by the French authority.

Later. Back at The Pips Headquarters. The Pips assemble at the Tennis Court. Watching the start of the second set between two of their investigators, Madison Allen, and Corrie Phelps. The score is tied.

Corrie Phelps serves up a hard one. Madison goes for the ball but fails to connect. Corrie is stoked. She serves again in the same spot.
RADIOS TRANSMITS…
DISPATCH: Body in a suitcase at Le Majestic on the Croisette in Cannes! Second floor - Room 202! Over!
Billy Black responds,
"That's a Copy!"
Corrie and Madison abort their game. Secure their rackets, and join HOTFOOT IT.

PREVIEW OF SEQUEL
BODY IN A SUITCASE

A woman from the backside, dressed in high heels and a green dress and flaunting her curves, strides while dragging a wheeled suitcase through an NYC Airport Parking Lot towards the Terminal. We do not see her face. Hours later, she arrives at Nice Airport in Southern France.

BODY IN A SUITCASE

FEATURING

THE PIPS

IN

MEDITERRANEAN PRIVATE EYE

SERIES

BY

JOHN ALAN ANDREWS

Copyright © 2024 by John A. Andrews

Books That Will Enhance Your Life

ISBN: 9798320733906

Cover Art: ALI

Cover Photo: ALI

All rights reserved.

BODY IN A SUITCASE

TABLE OF CONTENTS

CHAPTER ONE..118
CHAPTER TWO..121
CHAPTER THREE..124
CHAPTER FOUR...127
CHAPTER FIVE...129
CHAPTER SIX..132
CHAPTER SEVEN..134
CHAPTER EIGHT..137
CHAPTER NINE...140
CHAPTER TEN..143
CHAPTER ELEVEN...145
CHAPTER TWELVE...148
CHAPTER THIRTEEN...151
CHAPTER FOURTEEN...155
CHAPTER FIFTEEN..159
CHAPTER SIXTEEN..162
CHAPTER SEVENTEEN..165
CHAPTER EIGHTEEN...168
CHAPTER NINETEEN...172
CHAPTER TWENTY...177
CHAPTER TWENTY-ONE...180
CHAPTER TWENTY-TWO...183
CHAPTER TWENTY-THREE...186
CHAPTER TWENTY-FOUR..190
CHAPTER TWENTY-FIVE..193
CHAPTER TWENTY-SIX...196
CHAPTER TWENTY-SEVEN...198
CHAPTER TWENTY-EIGHT...201
CHAPTER TWENTY-NINE..204

CHAPTER ONE

It is a quiet evening in Suburban New York, except for a gentle breeze seen from the trees. As a result, their leaves die and fall to the ground. Meanwhile, some occasional vehicular traffic zooms by with lights at half-beam. Crickets creak, and their screech overlaps like muddled audio.
Inside the cul-de-sac duplex, left-over work documents crowd the four-seater dining table. To put it bluntly, the table is in complete disarray.

Seated amongst the shabby and examining cluster of paperwork, ABIGAIL CREIGHTON, a well-groomed Caucasian woman in her 40s, scrutinizes multiple correspondence documents. She seems pressurized but displays a façade of better days to come. Subsequently, she bites her lips. Her cell phone rings and goes unanswered.

On her laptop computer screen, scenic pictures of the Mediterranean reside unattended. Multiple framed legal awards decorations backdrop the wall. Two animated Goldfish in the mid-sized aquarium situated directly underneath the award portraits flip, chasing each other and gravel for food beneath the fish tank's rocky bottom.

Abigail glances up as GEORGE CREIGHTON, 40, ambulates downstairs. Abigail reacts to a whiff.

"New cologne? Late-night rendezvous?"

She asks,

"Grabbing a beer with the staff."

George replies. Rolling her eyes, Abigail is not buying his alibi.

"Two employees?"

She counters.

"A handful. Jeff, Michael, and the crew. You have met..."

George replies.

"Two is a company. There is a crowd."

States, Abigail.

"You can come if you want to."
Says George.
"Late invitation, George. You know I do not do well at the last minute."
Says Abigail.
George looks at the paperwork on the messy dining table and states:
"It looks like you brought the office home again tonight..."
Perusing additional documents, Abigail states," I am leaving for Southern France tomorrow, remember?"
Old news to George.
"Too many courtroom shenanigans... "
George sat and exited, hurried.
Abigail hums a tune and continues working.

CHAPTER TWO

An automobile engine cuts on, followed by a slammed car door. The car motors off with George in the driver's seat. Back at the house, Abigail stares at the Mediterranean Coastline on her laptop. After nursing a mood change, she grabs her car keys and bolts through the front door. Inside their garage, Abigail scoots inside a car. The front license tags read HERTZ. She cuts the engine on and slams the door hard. She was again biting her lips. The car whisks away. Abigail navigates the NYC suburban neighborhood like a P.I. She finds George's car parked outside a two-story Condo a few blocks away. Semi-darkness prevails. The top-floor bedroom is dimly lit. Abigail ponders her decision. Inside that room, oblivious to Abigail, George, and MELODY SMITH, in her 30s, on the bed, engage in foreplay. George, standing near the bed, moves towards her. They salivate for each other. She yearns for George. He craves her. Suddenly, Abigail sees their silhouettes. She took pictures on her cell phone in Paparazzi style until she had had enough. She steers her car away from the curb and makes a U-turn. Moments later, she returns home and immerses herself in additional document perusal at Melody's Condo. The front door opens and in walks NOAH SMITH, Melody's husband, 40s. Melody and George are now about to get naked and immediately change plans. Noah sees their advances and is irate. He threatens. George is over-apologetic and darts out. Noah reads Melody the riot act. George returns home. Abigail is alerted as the front door opens. He is semi-breathless. Abigail, still going through papers at her make-shift office, investigates... She is focused.

"Robust co-workers, George?"

"Yep. Those hires are a riot."

Abigail stares intensely at George.

"You now smell like... Atomic Rose."

A boiling Kettle whistles from the vicinity of the kitchen. She darts to the kitchen and attends to the whistling kettle. Meanwhile, George heading upstairs,

"Good night. Busy day tomorrow."

Abigail vowing to square the hole:

"Good night, George!"

CHAPTER THREE

Taking a break from the documents, Abigail opens the bedroom door. Inside, she sees George stretching out fast asleep and snoring. She returns downstairs, grabs her keys off the keyholder, and sneaks outside. Abigail jumps inside her car. It motors off. Later, she pulls up at Melody's Condo. She gets out and knocks on the door.
Inside: Melody watches TV from the bed – seminude.

"Hello. Who is this...? Noah? What happened to your keys? I thought you were already at the airport. Melody heads toward the door, puzzled.
Abigail is pressing up against the front door and pressing play on her iPhone app. From the gadget audio emits:
"George! George! This is George."
Melody opens the door and sticks her head outside, complaining:
"George, you will get me in trouble. What if Noah's flight gets canceled, and he returns home? Déjà vu!"
Abigail barges in, rope in hand. Clobbers Melody. Pushes her up against the other side of the door.
"You are already in trouble, B...!"
 She throws a lasso around Melody's neck and draws tightly on the rope, choking her to death. Melody collapses onto the floor. Abigail drags the body out to her car, throws her inside the trunk, slams it shut, and scoots inside on the driver's seat. The car motors off. Hours later, Abigail arrives at JFK Airport dragging her wheeled suitcase. She wheels up to the counter. The Baggage Attendant asks:
"Miss, are you carrying Lithium Batteries, Aerosol, or Coffee beans in your checked bag? "
"No Maam!"
Says Abigail.
The Attendant weighs the bag and puts it up on the carousel.

She successfully checked in the luggage. However, she was worried, wondering if the TSA would open and take a peek. Anyway, she proceeded and encountered an extended security check line.
"I hate delays. Lines? Synonymous with NYC!
Several TSA agents give her a second look, but none a third. Abigail tepidly saunters toward the gate with concern while staring at the departure boarding. It is loaded with canceled and delayed flights. She paces, an unhappy camper who now traverses the boarding area, peeved. Suddenly, her flight from JFK to Nice appears on the board, along with the gate number: ON TIME, it reads. Moments later, Abigail, poised to board, smiles gracefully.

CHAPTER FOUR

Back at Abigail's house, George tosses and turns in bed. He looks in the full-length mirror and dislikes himself. He reaches for his phone and dials Melody. He gets her voicemail. "This is Melody. You are not my only caller. So, leave a message."

George wishes it weren't so but responds, "Mel, this is George. Hi. You are out. Great News: Abigail is overseas. So, do you know what? I would love to have you over so we could kick it."

Rebounding, he toys with the phone, staring obsessively at Melody's cute picture. She is outfitted in a sexy green dress, much like the one Abigail wore to the airport. His phone rings. He is energized and expectant of Melody's return call. The caller ID reads Private.
"Hello. Hello. Hi. Hello!"
Yells, George.
No one answers.
He aborts the call, somewhat rattled about the non-identifier.
"Who was that? Another fraud call. Whatever are you selling? I am not buying. Not today, unless it is my sweet Melody, so sweet like the harp in any symphony."
The doorbell rings. George physically answers. There is no one. He is perturbed and throws a punch, which lands and creates a big hole in the wall. George recalibrates and scans the TV channels. He eventually parks on a movie with French subtitles.

CHAPTER FIVE

The Commercial Aircraft carrying Abigail Creighton lands at Nice Cote d'Azur airport. Abigail surveys cautiously and eventually joins the crowd of deplaned passengers. In cohesion, they hustle to the baggage claim and frequent the airline's carousel. Multiple suitcases resemble. Abigail, in a hurry, grabs a wheeled suitcase and wanders off. Other passengers follow suit. She arrives at Le Majestic in Cannes and enters hotel room #606. Displaying a sign of relief, she accesses her carry-on. Abigail removes a makeup pouch and lands it on the bathroom sink. She returns to her carry-on and fetches a pen and paper. Abigail writes a note: YOU WILL BURN IN HELL and is poised to insert that message in the suitcase. She meticulously opens the luggage. Aahhh… she echoes frantically. She finds it filled with menswear. Three neatly folded handkerchiefs are monogrammed – Noah Smith. Regaining her presence of mind, she erupts with laughter, rips up the note, and tosses it in the trash can. Rushing to the bathroom, she grabs a washcloth, dries her laughing tears, and looks at herself in the mirror. Her makeup bleeds. On the sink is, among other toiletries, her makeup case. She opened the makeup case and repaired the facial damage. She bursts out laughing.

"Ha-ha, Ha! This is so unbelievable. Someone else wanted to conduct the funeral…"

Her cell phone rings. She ignores it.

"Dust to dust, ashes to ashes. Now and forever, you will leave other women's husbands alone. Make sure YOU let her know!"

Meanwhile, Noah Smith, oblivious to Abigail, arrives at the Le Majestic Hotel. He checks into room #202. He gets ready to shower. He opens the suitcase. Inside: His wife Melody Smith's body is immovable. Noah, alarmed and hysterical: Help! What the F…? Somebody, help! Who did this?

Morons! Morons! Morons!" He hears his echo. Nobody responds.

Total Silence…

CHAPTER SIX

Finally, Noah realizes he has been talking to himself. Noah desists and rests his cheek on that of Melody's. He breaks down in tears.
"Why did someone do this? How am I going to explain this to these French Wasps?"
He eyes the phone on the nightstand. Mustering energy and courage, he calls 112. A dispatcher picks up the phone. Before a word is said: "Can I talk to the police?"

"Sir, be sure to maintain your calm. Are you hurt?" Ask the dispatcher.

"Hurt all right! Get me the darn police!"

"Sir. What is your name? Where are you located? And why do you need the police?"

"My name is Noah Smith. I just flew in from New York. I am at the Le Majestic Hotel, room 202. I picked up the wrong suitcase at baggage claim. A dead body is inside, and it is my freaking wife's! Someone is trying to incriminate me."

"Hang tight. Sir, Mr. Smith, Noah? The Pips are on their way..."

"The Pips?"

Noah asks

"Yes. The Paradise Investigation Protective Service. They will be on their way shortly. THE PIPS ARE AT A TENNIS COURT, and we are watching the beginning of the second set between two of their investigators, Madison Allen and Corrie Phelps. The score is tied: 13, 13. Corrie Phelps serves. It's a hard one. Madison goes for the ball and fails to connect. Corrie is stoked. Radios transmits.

"Dead body in a suitcase at Le Majestic! Room 202! Over!"

Corrie and Madison abort the game. They secure their tennis gear and hustle out behind the rest of The Pips. Sireen vehicles later form a dispatched con

CHAPTER SEVEN

Sirens crescendo. The Pips' convoy pulls up at Le Majestic Hotel. The Pips head up to room #202. They find Noah in tears and cold sweat. He greets.
"Thanks for showing up."
"My name is Billy Black, with the Pips. What is your name, sir?"
"My name is Noah Smith."

"Do you have an ID, Noah Smith?"
Noah reaches inside his pocket and presents his ID. Billy Black looks over Noah's credentials, eyed by the other Pips' squad. Billy Black asks,
"How may we assist you, Mr. Smith?"
Noah Smith replies.
"Mr. Black, I just flew in from New York JFK on business. I opened the luggage and discovered my wife's body inside.
"Whose body is in the suitcase?"
Billy Black asks.
"My wife's, Melody... Melody Smith."
Billy Black, still positioned in the crack of the room door.
"Who put her in the suitcase?"
"No idea. Come on inside. See for yourself!"
Billy Black trails Noah, followed by the other Pips in tow. The suitcase lies on the living room floor. Noah opens it hesitantly — Inside lies Melody's corpse. The Pips are startled.
"Your suitcase? How did this occur?"
Asks Billy Black.
"I was in a hurry and picked up this suitcase at baggage claim. It looked exactly like mine. So, I grabbed it,"
States, Noah Smith.
Billy Black shakes his head no.

"No one has yet to report this luggage mix-up." Noah opens his wallet and extracts a small white paper square. He peels off a baggage claim tag from it and hands it to Black.

Billy Black examines the tag. Again, he shakes his head in disbelief.

CHAPTER EIGHT

Noah feels the letdown and comes full circle.
"That is my luggage claim tag. It does not match the one on the bag."
Says Noah.
"That's right! Have you contacted the Airport's Lost and Found?"
"Yes, Mr. Black. I did so about an hour ago. It took me all that time before someone picked up the darn

phone. Then they could do nothing for me, and they kept talking to someone else in French."

Corie Phelps, the Red Head Girl, peers in and asks: "Mr. Smith, did you change the tag on your suitcase at baggage claim, or did someone switch your tags?"

Noah Smith seems confused. "Mr. Smith. While waiting for your luggage at the airport carousel, it can be challenging to identify your bag if it looks like other bags. One way to determine your bag, Mr. Smith, is to check the tag. The tag should contain your name, flight number, and destination airport code. This helps ensure that you pick up the correct bag. Did you switch the tags on your bag?"

Asks Billy Black.

"I was in a hurry. I did not think about such. No, I did not switch any tags. How do I get out of this?"

Billy Black states bluntly,

"Someone has been murdered. We're going to have to take you in for questioning."

Noah Smith is tense.

Vince Taylor places handcuffs on Noah Smith and escorts him outside. He puts Noah in the waiting cruiser.

Al Nobles collects necessary evidence, including biometrics. The Pips squad is in the driveway. They get ready to leave. The Paramedics' vehicle carrying Melody Smith's body drives away. French Police vehicles bear down. They swarm the driveway.

Investigator Welch steps out from one of their vehicles. Billy Black rolls down the driver's window.
"Mr. Welch, we have met again."
"Black, we heard that someone brought in a body in a suitcase."
Says Welch.
Billy Black responds,
"Welch, we very much have this under control."
"Really. Do you?"
"You can read my lips. We have got this."
Welch insists.
Billy Black states candidly.
The cruiser carrying Noah Smith motors off. Investigator Welch looks at his outmatched squad.
"Too late."
Welch and his team beeline, boards, and motor off, contrariwise.
Billy Black's auto sends exhaust smoke on Welch's auto's tail.

CHAPTER NINE

Oblivious to the previous legal maneuvers at Le Majestic, Abigail Creighton, dressed in a jogging suit, is poised for a jog. Even so, she noticed the crime scene's yellow tape fluttering with the wind but gave it little attention or linkage to herself. So caught up in herself, Abigail looks over in the hotel lobby's glass window, then briskly hits the streets en route to the trails for her pre-sunset workout.

AT THE SAME TIME, AT A NEW YORK AIRPORT, The American Airlines Airplane touches down. Accompanied by a convoy of two NYPD cruisers, The Pips arrive at Smith's New York home. Aided by two NYPD Officers. The NYPD Uniformed Officer DALE JACOBS rings the doorbell at George and Abigail Creighton's home. The other NYPD officer, Marc Santos, establishes his presence at the rear along with The Pips. They waited for someone to answer the door after multiple ringing of the doorbell. Eventually, George Creighton shows up. He is startled as he notices badged officers at his door and the two NYPD vehicles parked in front of his driveway. However, George Creighton refuses to let them in.
"What can I do for you?"
George asks.
The NYPD Officer, Dale Jacobs, responds,
"Mr. Creighton, my name is Officer Dale Jacobs with the NYPD. We need to ask you a few questions about your wife, Abigail. Do you mind if we come in?"
George is petrified as he looks at the team of investigators in waiting. George asks, "...and who are those other guys?"
Dale Jacobs responds:
"Mr. Creighton, we are accompanying The Pips, a team of investigators from the Mediterranean based in Southern France."

George is open-mouthed. However, they still show reluctance.

CHAPTER TEN

The Neighbors across the street are out of their houses and on the sidewalk. They eavesdrop. Dale Jacobs senses George's staged delay. From the folder in his possession, he pulls out and reads the search warrant to George Creighton.
"We would like to accompany you on a house tour." Says Dale Jacobs after reading the warrant.
"Sure."
They are permitted to enter and proceed to rummage. Still shell-shocked and discombobulated,

George accommodates. The investigative delegation's five men and three women entered Creighton's house. The door closed behind them. George leads the way upstairs. The Pips and NYPD trails. They visit the two bedrooms. Vince Taylor takes pictures.

Billy Black eyes Dale Jacobs.

Seeking corroboration: Dale Jacobs also eyes objects in the living room and its perimeter. So do The Pips.

"Your wife went to France, didn't she? "

Asks Jacobs. George ponders as if he does not know about his wife's trip.

"Did she or did she not go to France?"

"Yes."

Dale Jacobs announces.

"Mr. Billy Black heads up the Pips investigative team and has questions for you."

"Abigail. She is okay, right?"

George asks.

"We are not sure about Mrs. Creighton. Didn't she contact you?"

Billy Black digs further. George postures and then responds,

"No."

"Mr. Creighton, how long has your wife Abigail been gone?"

"A little over five days."

George says.

CHAPTER ELEVEN

Billy Black ponders.
"Did she tell you where she was going?" "Yes. France, Southern France. I believe that is where she went to." Billy Black, ignoring the shenanigans, "How long has she been planning this trip, and why were you not invited to tag along?"
"More than a month."
"Did she ever suggest your accompaniment, or did she prefer to take the trip alone?"

Asks Billy Black.

"She wanted to be alone."

"Do you know why she wanted to do so?"

"Abigail cherishes her independence. She said she needed a much-desired vacation. "

"Do you know of a woman named Melody Smith?" Asks Billy Black.

"No. Never heard of her."

Scratching his head, Billy Black asks:

"Have you ever heard of Melody Smith?"

"What I've said is correct. I do not know who you are talking about."

Vince Taylor hands Billy Black his camera and a slide show of pictures copied from portraits of Melody taken earlier at the condominium. Billy Black indulges George Creighton's recollection.

"Never met that woman. Not my type." Billy Black, staring into George Creighton's soul,

"Really?"

Across the way, Vince Taylor ensues lifting fingerprints from the door and surrounding areas. Bingo. He notices a woman's fingernail on the floor, colored pink. He picks it up and enters evidence. Meanwhile, Billy Black, Yovanda Nichols, Corrie Phelps, Madison Allen, Vince Taylor, and Ralph Gomez rummage through individual rooms in search of corroborating evidence. The two NYPD officers stand back but in overseeing mode. Billy

Black proceeds to the living room. There on the couch, in front of the active TV showing the movie The French Connection, Billy Black retrieves an iPhone and briskly puts it into evidence.

"Mr. Creighton, is there a basement or garage?"

Asks Billy Black.

"There is a garage."

Says George Creighton. "Please, will you lead us to that garage?"

Billy Black asks.

George seems hesitant but does. The agents follow in earnest.

CHAPTER TWELVE

Billy Black is focused on not only drilling but also squaring the hole. He points...
"Mr. Creighton, the garage."
George reluctantly leads the way. George's car is parked on one side. The other parking space is vacant. A paper car mat liner, which reads HERTZ, lingers. Noticing the parked car.
"Whose car?"
Asks Billy Black.

"That is my car. Where is all this going?"
"Who killed Melody Smith? Did you share this car with Abigail?
"No."
"What does Abigail drive?"
"She recently drove a rental. Why all these questions?"
"Melody Smith has been murdered. We are trying to find out who committed the murder and why."
States, Corie Phelps, aka the Redhead Girl investigator.
"I have nothing to do with anyone's murder."
George interjects. Corrie Phelps notices a paper car mat liner on the ground. She retrieves and turns it over. HERTZ is also printed on both sides in Bold block letters. She locks in Billy Black's attention.
"Abigail must have rented it from Hertz."
Billy Black stares at George questioningly.
"She rented it from Hertz. Did she or didn't she?"
Before George could answer, Vince Taylor discovered a rope on the floor.
Billy Black points to the dangling rope in Vince Taylor's hand.
"The same one that Abigail used to strangle Melody Smith?"
Asks Ralph Gomez, while Vince Taylor enthusiastically captures multiple pictures of the rope and enters them into evidence. Billy Black nods

YES at Vince Taylor. Members of the Pips' team, as well as the two NYPD officers, observe. They feel at this point that they have landed on substantial evidence. However, Billy Black craves more. "Did Abigail disclose where she was lodging in Southern France?"

"Abigail is known for her covert operations. Sorry." Says George.

"Mr. Creighton, were you truthful when you said you did not realize Melody Smith?"

Asks Corie Phelps.

"I never met or knew of anyone with that name."

Mr. Creighton, we tend to believe that you do. But if you said you do not. We will have you come to the Precinct for biometric evidence."

Says Billy Black.

"Are you trying to arrest me for not knowing someone? Really?"

"Not really. It is part of our investigation. Please do not obstruct our investigation, Mr. Creighton."

Billy Black says,

George reluctantly accommodates. The NYPD officer shoves George into the cruiser's rear seat, and the three-car-convoy motors off.

CHAPTER THIRTEEN

Back in Cannes, near the Crossette, Abigail, dressed in a jogging suit, returns to room #606 at Le Majestic. She mops her forehead, sits on the couch, and turns on the TV in desperation. The Cannes Confidential show is on.

"We interrupt this program with late - Commercial breaking news. It was reported three days ago that the body of an American woman, Melody Smith, was discovered in a suitcase after her husband, Noah

Smith, called 112 regarding him picking up the wrong suitcase at the Nice Airport. The Pips, an investigative Mediterranean French agency, was dispatched to the Hotel where her husband, Mr. Noah Smith, was lodging and discovered the corpse of Mrs. Smith in a suitcase. Mr. Smith denied the allegations but has since been arrested for additional questioning. In related news, according to sources, the Pips, aided by the NYPD, also met and interviewed the husband of Abigail Creighton in New York."

States, the Newscaster. Abigail, watching the news, is frenetic.

"More to come on this unfolding story,"

The newscaster concludes, and the Network returns to its regular programming. Abigail turns off the TV. She fetches bottled water and goes to the deck. Cannes Islands are in the foreground, peaking.

Abigail paces restlessly.

"Darn! What must he have told them? George was never like this. He has become such a loser. I hope that he did not tell them where I was staying."

Her phone rings. She checks the ID. It says private. She hesitates but answers anyway.

INTERCUTING between Abigail Creighton and the badgered husband, George Creighton.

"Gail, what the heck are you doing? By sending Police from France to investigate me...?"

"George, why are you calling me on a private line...?"

"Cause I am under surveillance at the precinct doing biometrics and using someone else's phone. If you wanted a divorce, you should ask for one instead of trying to do me in..."

"Well, George, seeing you raised the scenario. Yes, I want a divorce, and you are going to freaking pay for it... all of it."

George tries lowering the temperature but puts salt into the wound:

"The Pips, you allegedly sent from France to investigate me, claimed you could have something to do with Melody Smith's disappearance..."

"Your lover, George?" "Her brother Jeff works for my company. He will freak out when he finds out what you did." "Was it he who introduced you to his happily married sister?

George maintains his silence.

"Well, You and he should have heard it in the news!"

"You know I do not watch the news."

George says.

"You should! Change is uncomfortable. I guess you have now found your way to the kitchen or survive on Ramen Noodles.

"Gail, I swear, you are going to regret this."
At the same time, A LATINEX WOMAN, uniformed and with a broom, moves towards George.
"Senior, I am going to need the use of my phone. My husband will call any minute. He is a very jealous man."
There's a knock on Abigail's room door.
Abigail is startled by such action.
The Knocker, a guest from next door, yells.
"Miss, could you lower your voice, please?"
Abigail attends with the phone in hand. She opens the door, and the Hotel Security joins the Knocker in a circular pacing frenzy.
Abigail continues verbally tearing George apart. The whooping escalates. It is too much for the Guest and Hotel Staff. They walk away. "You should call the cop. No woman talks to me that way. I don't care one bit about her Academic status.
Seeing the *keepers of the peace* leave gives Abigail a creative license to dig into George.
"George, were you threatening me? Was that supposed to be a threat?"
"You figure it out..." George gives the finger to the atmosphere and hands the phone to the Hispanic Woman. He bounces, leaves Abigail hanging, and catches an NYC Yellow Taxi.

CHAPTER FOURTEEN

Abigail embarks on another jogging binge. She explores immediate Cannes locations with frequent stops, including boutiques, shooting ranges, and eateries. Continuing her jog, she finds the strip mall with a nail salon. Elated, she pops in and repairs her damaged fingernail. Subsequently, Abigail jogs her way back to the Gun Shop. She is tickled upon entering the front door. The GUN SHOP OWNER, a middle-aged Frenchman, provides her with an application. She quickly fills it out and returns it with a facade. The Gun Shop Owner runs her credentials and stalls the sale.

"Miss, I'm sorry, but according to the information you provided, you do not qualify for concealed or open carry."

Abigail is antsy. "What do you mean?" "Sorry, I am unable to bend the rules." "Like they say in Jamaica: No Problem, and in Howard Beach: No Problema." Abigail says and bounces, unaccomplished. Later. Abigail Creighton shows up at the local shooting range and embarks on honing her shooting skills. She misses a few but hits most of them in the bull's-eye. Abigail takes a break. She flexes her limbs, grabs a bottle of water from the snack machine, tosses it into the air, catches it on the fallback, pops the cork, takes a swig, then a guzzle, and gets set to return to the range. MILES MATTERSON, a middle-aged Frenchman posted at the front counter and previously eyeing the surveillance monitor, gets her attention. He smiles.

"Hey, you missed some of your shots, huh? Keeping your eyes off the target? It happens with most beginners. Hang in there. Soon, you will get it, Miss New Yorker."

"How did you know where I'm from…? I forgot I gave you my info. By the way, that was done on purpose with the gun. Just in case I did not want to hurt someone badly but wanted to give them a chance to survive through all their pains."

"Really? Most people from New York shoot to kill. I am saying that despite my New York affiliation, I love options. Taking someone out is never an issue for me. I can fake it, and I can bake it. Back there, I chose to fake it."

Says Abigail, non-apologetically.

"Sorry, but I have been here for ten years. Seen a variety of shooters. I must say, I am not quickly sold."

"Have it your way, Miles. I can shoot to kill in a heartbeat."

With that mindset, Abigail returns to the shooting mound. She pops new clips into the gun and SHOOTS, hitting each target in a different area Then she alternates: She clips one in the groin, the next in the lungs, the next in the heart, one in both eyes, and the next in the skull. Erratically, She reloads. Faster than before, she hits the entire body - firing shot after shot until the target dissipates into debris. She is satisfied. While watching her shooting drill on the surveillance monitor, Miles Matterson is tepid but applauds anyway.

"She's got skills."

He says under his breath. After that sprint, Abigail prepares to leave and returns her shooting gear.

"Miles, do you know where I can purchase here in Cannes?"
She asks.
"There is a Gun Shop a few blocks west on the Croisette.
Abigail vividly remembers that "no sale" joint.
"Forget them, Miles. I need a hot purchase. Like last week."
"Be careful, little hands, what you do. I used to sing that in Sunday School…Now, you are trying to get both of us into trouble. You may want to try Antibes; there is less red tape there. However, you may not use me as your referral. We have never met. Got it?"
"Got it! Thanks."
Abigail hustles.

CHAPTER FIFTEEN

At The Pips Headquarters, investigators toy with assorted NYC souvenirs. One, in particular, is a suitcase with a key ring attached. Al Nobles walks in, clutching a manila folder under his armpit. It reads Biometrics. Investigators, eyes peeled.
Billy Black tosses Al that NYC souvenir. Al catches it like a football thrown by a Quarterback. He appreciates the gesture. The Pips cheer on Al Noble's catch.

"Thanks. Welcome back, guys."
Says Al Nobles.
"Thanks, Al. What is the temperature with Mr. Smith and that body in the suitcase? Are we moving the needle at the labs?"
"Based on my tenure as an experienced investigator, I must say: It does not look good for his alibi; he failed the polygraph test. Plus, according to the coroner's report, His wife died from affixation, ruling out that a rope could have been the weapon of choice. Allegedly, her murderer must have used that option to avoid leaving any blood trails. Plus, his biometrics were lifted from inside that suitcase. The evidence he is somewhat connected."
"Double jeopardy...? That accounts for the rope discovered inside the garage at the residence of Abigail and George Creighton. Her husband, George, could have been having an affair with Melody Smith – the body in that suitcase. Although he failed to admit such and even said he didn't know who she was."
"Failure to recall? Somebody is lying... According to our findings, The broken fingernail of a woman was found at the home of Noah and Melody Smith, where the murder occurred. Then her body could have been transported to the killer's house, where the rope was discovered... A fight ensued;

fingernails aren't broken so easily. There is some there, there."

"The body was packed in the suitcase and rushed to the airport as part of the killer's checked luggage."

States, Madison Allen.

"A love triangle? This is beginning to make sense. The transporter of the body from New York allegedly killed Melody, moved the body to her house, then to the airport, and checked it onto the airplane. Then, when it arrived in France, there was a luggage mix-up, and accidentally, ironically, the husband of the victim claimed that suitcase at the baggage claim."

States, Al Nobles.

"That pocket edition has merit. The Love Triangle. Sold!"

Says Billy Black as if he hit a home run in the case.

CHAPTER SIXTEEN

The look on Corie Phelp's face suggests she is digging more deeply into this investigation.
"Abigail Creighton's fingerprints seem to be all over this murder. She must have been pressed for time to dispose of the body properly and opted to bring it with her to a foreign country and get rid of it then. Thus, leaving no trace of the murder... back there in New York."
Says Corie Phelps. "If her husband had checked the darn tag on his bag... Didn't he listen to the announcement from Baggage Claim?"

Phelps smiles at his gesture. Giving thumbs up on the inside. "If Abigail still has his suitcase...? Is she wearing his stuff?"
Asks Yovanda Nichols.
"Maybe."
Says Phelps.
"What if there is also a dead body in his suitcase, which was claimed by her?"
Asks Madison Allen.
"She would have been too scared to report it."
States Al Nobles. Corie Phelps interjects:
"That has a comedic edge to it. Doesn't it?"
They all chuckle at those preceding remarks, except for Billy Black. He remains poker-faced.
"Let's hit the road. Find Abigail Creighton and put a button on this."
Says Billy Black.
His phone rings. He answers it.
"This is Billy Black."
For a moment, there's silence on the phone. Billy Black listens and relays:
"So, he is being remanded in custody. Okay. Indefinitely? Got you."
"George Creighton is?"
Asks Phelps. Billy Black to The Pips:
"On the contrary. Noah Smith is remanded in custody to allow forensic evidence to be thoroughly

investigated. Which means his release is indefinite."
Phelps asks.
"So, where does that leave us in the dark?"
Billy Black ponders:
"Turn on the flashlight. Let us find Abigail Creighton. They might disagree, but she lines up as our ultimate target." "Another Manhunt in Paradise?"
Asks Phelps.
"This time, it is Body In A Suitcase. And according to her husband, this is her maiden voyage to France. Unless she is lodging with a French local, she is bound to face multiple hurdles in acclimating to the area. She is about to experience this, but it is not the U.S." "Survival for the misfit or the fittest?"
Asks Al Nobles.
"Unless she takes a crash course in French and knows her way around the city, she is severely handicapped."
States, Billy Black.
The Pips hit the streets in separate vehicles.

CHAPTER SEVENTEEN

Billy Black pulls up outside the Gun Shop visited by Abigail Creighton the day before. In the window, a CLOSED black sign with white lettering dangles from two strings. Meanwhile, in another window, a posted sign reads closed at 7:00 PM daily. He meets the GUN SHOP OWNER, who is set to lock up for the end of the day. Billy Black is resilient and flashes his badge. The Gun Shop Owner sees him and emerges, creating a slight crack in the front door.
"Hi sir, how are you?"

Billy Black asks.

The Gun Shop Owner points to the CLOSED sign in the store window.

"Sorry. We are closed for the day."

It seems like you were closed earlier than usual. States, Billy Black.

"I reserve that right. Don't you think?"

"Is that the way you treat your prospective clients?" Billy Black asks.

"On a good day, no. On a dreadful day, yes. It's a Family business. I need to get going."

Says the Gun shop Owner.

Black presses:

"I am Billy Black with the Pips investigative team."

"Mr. Black, I know who you are."

"Thanks. Did you supply an American woman with ammunition during the last week?"

Asks Billy Black.

"Sorry. I do not discuss my clients or potential clients with anyone. Not even law enforcement, unless subpoenaed. Once again, I am dealing with a family emergency and cannot host an interview. What happens in my Gun Shop stays in my Gun Shop, Mr. Black."

The Gun Shop Owner boards his SUV and takes off. Billy Black gets inside his car and does the same, but contrariwise. He is enjoying hip-hop music from his favorite station. In the interim, his radio transmits and is voiced by the Dispatch.

"A young woman was shot at the Parc Phoenix Park. Over!" Billy Black's car makes a swift U-turn. Its Sirens crescendo as it races towards the Park. Sirens echo as Ambulances take shortcuts towards the Park. Moving vehicles gives the right way on the streets.

CHAPTER EIGHTEEN

Billy Black pulls up at the shooting range's parking lot. Al Nobles waits in the car. He acknowledges Black's arrival with a thumbs up. Billy Black responds kindly. Billy Black exits his car and heads for the main door. Al Nobles, surveys. Billy Black enters the shooting range full of passion and purpose. He surveys. Few adrenaline-rushed patrons make their exits.

At the counter, the middle-aged attendee Miles Matterson greets:

"How are you? Are you joining us today to work out or for lessons? If it is for the latter, can you return tomorrow? Our Coach has been out sick for days."

"Sorry to hear. Neither. I am here because one of your clients could be in serious trouble."

Miles Matterson is reserved as Black digs.

"Have a name?"

"Abigail Creighton."

"Got you! Well, sir, what is your name?"

"Billy Black, with the Pips. Have you seen her?" "It sounds like you are recreating a musical album."

"Don't get this twisted."

"You guys have become popular lately. More so since the arrest of that Aziz Michael."

Billy Black absorbs the compliment.

"Thanks."

Billy Black takes a beat, looking into Miles Matterson's soul.

"Fill me in. I do not want to have to subpoena records, but if we must, we will."

Miles Matterson buoys up.

"Mr. Black, you must talk with the owner about any legal issues. I work here. I sign in and sign out. Who comes and goes is my business. However, it remains none of my business. Do you understand my drift?"

"For a while, I thought you were a man of a few words. What's the owner's name?"

Miles Matterson reflects. While assimilating Billy Black's satire. "Aziz Michael."

"Now you are playing me; that ship sailed already, Miles Matterson." "A guy like you ought to be able to take a joke."

States, Miles Matterson.

Billy Black goes to his iPhone and displays a picture. "Abigail Creighton. Have you seen her here?"

"As I have told you, Mr. Black. It is my business, but still not mine, regarding whoever enters through these doors. I see nothing. I hear nothing but rent Amo and collect them when they are done with them."

Billy Black reads the looks on Miles Matterson's guilty face.

"When was the last time she was here?"

He asks.

"Yesterday, before noon."

Miles Matterson, responds.

"Miles, if you see her again, give us a call. Will you?" Asks Billy Black.

"I will see what I can do to help. Please understand that everything I have divulged is entirely off the record. I hope you did not record our conversation, Mr. Black."

States, Miles Matterson.

"I would have asked... and remember, one hand washes the other."

Billy Black gives Miles Matterson a business card and leaves in haste.

Miles Matterson yells:

"Black! It is said another way. You scratch my back, and I'll scratch yours."

Black glances at him peripherally but does not slow his posture.

CHAPTER NINETEEN

Billy Black's auto pulls into the driveway at Le Majestic Hotel. Guests frequent the exterior. Billy Black exits the car, focused. He gets second looks from some guests, but most minding their business. A valet steps up and parks the auto. Heading towards the front door, Billy Black meets SMOOTH JOE coming out. "Hey, Black, I saw when you rolled up." Billy Black, jokingly, "Does everybody have the same prerogative?"

Smooth Joe, missing the jest,
"Why do you ask?" "When a criminal sees me, I prefer to be pointing my gun at them and not them pointing theirs at me."
"This is Cannes, not the Wild, Wild, West. There have been no criminals up here since Aziz. Look around, have it your way."
Says Smooth Joe.
"I might just take you up on that. My hunch is a kicker. Frank Sinatra said: I did it my way."
"This is not Monday-night football at Le Majestic."
Says Smooth Joe.
"We did drag Noah Smith out of here a few days ago. Why would a man do such a thing?"
Asks Billy Black.
"I do not believe he did it, Black."
Says, Smooth Joe.
"Do you have any evidence to support his innocence?"
The two men sit at a table. The host serves Smooth Joe, his favorite Heineken, and Billy Black Perrier Water.
"Sounds like a setup. He must have been that flash-in-the-pan the killer wanted."
States, Smooth Joe.
"Really? What if the killer spends time here?"
Asks Billy Black.
Smooth Joe ignores the question.

"Do I need an NDA in place to get on board?"
"Something like that."
Billy Black shows him a pic of Abigail Creighton. "Have you seen her?"
"Sounds like the Chi-Lites, Black. The song was released on May 27, 1972. Sold over one million copies and was awarded a gold disc by the RIAA. "
Says, Smooth Joe.
"Thompson, Lester, and Jones recorded their first charting song, "Give It Away" written by Davis and Record. That came first from the 1960s to the 1970s."
Billy Black counters.
"Do I need to draw from the Black Music Encyclopedia to get the gig?"
Smooth Joe insists.
"Do not play me. That, Smooth Joe, is for you to figure out. Not for me to enact. What did HR say?"
The waitress serves them a round of their favorite drinks and departs.
"Said: Not sure I could be trusted with a gun and authority."
Asks Billy Black.
"Really?"
Asks Smooth Joe.
"Sounded like it came from Guess Who?"
Asks Billy Black.
"Aristotle? Ernest Hemingway? Al Capone?"

"Bob Marley sang: Who the cap fit wears it."
States Smooth Joe sarcastically.
Billy Black responds.
"He sure did, along with "Bend down low."
Smooth Joe, changing the conversation:
"How much are you and your guys willing to pay? Understanding I am putting myself in harm's way without carrying a gun."
"That's up for a vote."
"Do not worry, Black. If the jogger comes through, I will let you know."
States, Smooth Joe. He thinks hard about the character, and continues:
"The Jogger?"
He ponders: "Yep, Abigail. If a woman has the intestinal fortitude, besides giving birth, to put her husband's lover in a suitcase, she must be a full-fledged sprinter. It is going to take everything the Pips to catch her... Black. That woman has the wind beneath her wings and is flying high with two guns."
Billy Black's phone rings. He takes the call.
"Okay. Okay, I got it."
Billy Black tells Smooth Joe:
"Thanks for your astrological input and a replay of Top Gun and Two-Gun Crowley; my favs. Call me if you see something or hear something. No ifs, and, or buts. Just the plain facts. Got to bring this home.
Billy Black bounces with a swagger.

Smooth Joe chews hard on the matter at hand.

CHAPTER TWENTY

Six members of the Pips busied inside The Pips Headquarters. Ralph Gomez surfs the Web next to Redhead Girl. Vince Taylor and Al Noble are focused on the biometrics of Noah Smith, George Creighton, and Abigail Creighton. Yovanda Nichols and Madison Allen share info gathered on Madison's iPad. Billy Black walks in, focused. The team drops their assignments and presses toward him, forming a huddle.

"Guys, we have already accomplished much. Thank you. However, until we catch Abigail Creighton, we have a huge task ahead of us. Since arriving in France, she has been training on how to fight us. For example, not only has Abigail Creighton been training at a shooting range, but she has also been on a jogging regiment."

"Really?"

Asks Yovanda Nichols, flexing her muscles. Billy Black continues:

"She exercises daily, according to one source, and the shooting range is her favorite hangout. We must hunt her down by giving this venture nothing but our best. The best police procedural tactics we can muster apply to this task."

"Do we need to expand our team to pull this off?"

Asks Ralph Gomez.

"We are built to win. I have always believed it is not the dog's size in the fight. It is the size of the fight in the dog."

Says Billy Black.

Al Nobles feel challenged. "We are equipped. We just must believe it, eat it, breathe it, and sleep it. We caught Aziz Michael, didn't we..."

Yovanda Nichols paces. "We have enough on Abigail Creighton to bring her down. That girl has nothing on any one of us."

Madison Allen is not a happy camper and shows her disgust.

"That is right. She does not. We have the goods on her. Except where she dwells. Is it Cannes, Nice, or Monaco? Once this becomes clear, we need to concentrate our efforts. We did that in Monaco when we apprehended Aziz Michael. "

"We did. And just like that, he was in custody. I am up to the challenge. Bring it on!"

Vows, Corie Phelps.

CHAPTER TWENTY-ONE

After listening to everyone's viewpoint, Billy Black weighs in.
"Bring it on, yes. We remain the most formidable investigators on land, air, sea, and underground. Neither obstructionists nor antagonists can defeat us. I must find out where her base camp is, and after that, we are going in." "Do we want her dead or alive?"

Asks Corie Phelps, the Redhead Girl.
"Alive is always better, but we will take what we get. If she pushes the needle, we have no choice but to take her out."
Billy Black instructs the team.
"We are The PIPS!"
Says Vince Taylor.
"Tomorrow is ours!"
Says Billy Black.
The Redhead Girl checks her gun.
"Yep!"
Billy Black's iPhone rings. He attends.
"Billy Black!"

INTERCUTING between Billy Black on the phone, the excited Smooth Joe, and ready for action - Vince Taylor.
"Black, your target checked in here two weeks ago but under a different name."
Says Smooth Joe.
"How legit are your sources?"
Billy black asks:
"Extraordinarily strong."
Says, Smooth Joe.
"I should have known. I felt the hunch and will take the hit. Okay, moving forward, keep your eyes peeled. We are coming in. The Pips overhear the

command and assemble themselves for the hunt."
Billy Black reminds The Pips,
"Cannes, it is!"

CHAPTER TWENTY-TWO

While they are getting ready to launch their pursuit of Abigail Creighton in Cannes, Late Breaking internal news drops.

"Hey, guys. News just in. You must see this!"

Yells, Vince Taylor.

Suddenly, their gathering is dissolved. Eight of them flock to Vince Taylor's office. He is locked into what's on his computer. Footage also overflows on the overhead monitor. It is footage from the Park

Phoenix shooting that involved the Gun Shop Owner's daughter, Destiny. In it, Abigail Creighton, wearing a jogging suit, is depicted firing the shot from close range, which cuts down Destiny. "Senseless shooting. What did that girl do?"
States, Billy Black.
"Her dad is a Gun Dealer. What if her dad refused to sell Abigail Creighton a gun or the type she wanted?"
States, Vince Taylor.
"I can see that."
Says Billy Black.
"Are those the first pictures of her since landing in Nice?"
Asks Yovanda Nichols.
"Yep. To my knowledge. Where has Abigail Creighton been hiding out?"
Questions, Madison Allen.
"That jogging suit character could have been seen in Cannes and Cannes Islands according to Smooth Joe."
States, Billy Black.
"Smooth Joe? Can he be relied on?"
Asks Yovanda Nichols.
"Do not rule him out, Nichols. He keeps his eyes peeled. According to sources, he hardly sleeps. We received a great tip from our guy in Monaco, remember?"

Says Madison Allen.

"Get your sleep, team. Let us see what we find in Cannes when the sun comes up. Jogging suits are in with a jacket to hide your details."

Says Billy Black.

"So, we are going jogging? Mr. Black, you are so undercover. Is that why you spend time together with Smooth Joe?"

Asks Yovanda Nichols,

"A strong possibility. He so would like to join our team except…? Yes, that is what it will take to find this killer. Nichols, you are adept at camouflage. A chapter from your playbook could certainly work to our advantage."

Says Billy Black.

Yovanda Nichols responds,

"Count me in!"

CHAPTER TWENTY-THREE

In the interim, Noah Smith returns to Le Majestic with a duffel bag and returns to Room #202. He checks the entire room, looking through every closet, the mini refrigerator, and even under the desk. Nothing to see. He opens the small duffel bag and highlights clothing items: two pairs of jeans, underwear, sports shirts, sneakers, and a dress shirt. He pulls back the window shade to let some sunshine in. Outside in an open dumpster, he notices a suitcase filled with menswear, including three neatly folded handkerchiefs, monogrammed - Noah. He quickly accesses his cell phone and, in Paparazzi style, captures some flicks. He is antsy for smoke. The non-smoking sign inside the room on the dresser looms. Smoke deprived. He grabs his wallet, his cell phone, a cigarette lighter, and a pack of cigarettes. He exits outside. Private cars, taxis, and other vehicles traverse the driveway.

The concierge team and parking attendants rotate. Noah lights up a cigarette and takes a well-desired puff. Suddenly, he is routed behind the head by a woman wearing a jogging suit. He goes down and tries to get up. She allows him to get back up. Abigail, the villain, waits for a BEAT, letting Noah Smith know he no longer intimidates her. Plus, she is armed and dangerous, with two guns protruding from underneath her jacket. Additionally, she fends off those hotel employees. Noah goes down.

To torture Noah, she kicks him hard in the gut. He goes back down. Noah sees the woman's face but does not know her identity. Guests, security personnel, and other hotel employees dare aid Noah. Noah, while down, futilely tries to grab the attacker with her feet. Abigail draws two guns from underneath her jacket and aims at Noah Smith. Secondly, the security personnel eventually mustered enough courage to confront the attacker –

Abigail, with his two waving batons. They back off. Smooth Joe, the Frenchman and ally of Billy Black pounces on the scene. He is thunderstruck and yells: "That is her. Abigail Creighton!"

Multiple onlookers hustle and bustle. In that commotion, A WOMAN on the hotel staff yells!

"No. That is Amelia Triton. I checked her in last week. Unless she bought that driver's license in Paris, which she displayed upon check-in."

"That is her. Abigail Creighton. She brought in that dead woman inside the suitcase. Debbie, that woman lied to you. That is not who she said she is."

Those remarks from Smooth Joe now draw a crowd. Multiple gunshots ring out, cutting down Noah Smith and injuring the front desk Woman - Debbie Clarke. Noah, unable to withstand another blow from Abigail, staggers, falls to the ground and collapses. One round intended for Smooth Joe misses him. She tries to get another off. CLICK! CLICK! CLICK!

The gun is out of bullets. Smooth Joe avoids that intended subsequent round and comes at her with a vengeance. Abigail Creighton sees him peripherally coming at her; no time to reload her gun, she jumps in the waiting limousine. It takes off speedily. SIRENS CRESCENDO AMBULANCES BEAR DOWN FRENCH POLICE VEHICLES BEAR DOWN The Croisette has suddenly become a rambunctious traffic parking lot dominated by emergency vehicles. Smoke from exhaust emissions saturates the atmosphere, while Noah's body's plasma is emitted.

CHAPTER TWENTY-FOUR

That getaway limousine vanished from the area before the Pips arrived in separate vehicles. They jump out wearing jogging gear. Billy Black notices and huddles with the animated, shaken-up Smooth Joe. "That B....! She got away. Tried to shoot me!" Billy Black hustles back toward his car. He reaches for the door. His cell phone rings. He answers. "This is Black."

The Gun Shop Owner is on the phone.

"I know you must be busy fighting crime. Destiny could not hold on any longer. We will bury her tomorrow."

The rest of the Pips huddle close to Billy Black in eavesdropping mode. The Gun Shop Owner continues,

"She passed away earlier today. I hope you catch that woman, or someone else will."

Billy Black responds,

"Sir, accept our condolences. We will do our best. Taking care of some police business at the moment."

Billy Black engages The Pips:

"That was Destiny's dad. Destiny did not make it."

Corrie Phelps is shaken and tears up. Madison Allen and Yovanda Nichols comfort her.

Investigator Welch emerges.

"Black, you did it again. This time it is an American, just like you, whose blood got spilled. Is that classified as a hate crime?" Redhead Girl regains her state of mind. "Mr. Welch, no disrespect but I wish you would just back off and let us do what we are assigned to do.

"I can see you have bought into their culture. Haven't you?"

Says Welch.

"Show us some footage, Welch."

Says Billy Black.

The Pips depart in multiple vehicles. In the background, Smooth Joe waves goodbye to Billy Black and The Pips.

"Be sure to catch her Mr. Black."

The convoy motors off from Le Majestic's driveway. It hits the road via The Croisette.

CHAPTER TWENTY-FIVE

Back in New York. The NYPD officers Dale Jacobs and Marc Santos returned with chains and locks to secure Smith's residence. While completing the inventory of the property, they notice a male's body hanging by a rope with its noose affixed to his neck. They investigate. In his seat pocket, they discover a wallet. Inside the wallet, they see a driver's license linked to the identity of the corpse. It is George

Creighton, lifeless, and hanging from that roof. He is dressed in a midnight blue, red, and white sweatsuit, and a pair of white sneakers – symbolic of the French colors. They also discovered his cell phone clasped tightly in his left hand. The phone – void of battery life.

"What the heck is going on?"

Asks Marc Santos.

"Looks like a Love Square. More than a triangle to me."

Says Dale Jacobs,

" George Creighton? We were over at his house last week with a search warrant. Remember, he vowed he did not know Melody Smith. Now he is hanging from the roof of her house – dead."

Marc Santos recounts.

"Saying he did not recall would have been better. Now he looks like he hanged himself above all places - in her bedroom."

Says Dale Jacobs, checking his temperature.

"He has been dead for some time; his body is cold as ice."

Jacobs gets on his radio. At the same time, Marc Santos captures pictures of the crime scene.

"A dead body was discovered hanging from the roof inside the Smith's master bedroom at 1017 New Hyde Park. The Characteristics match those of George Creighton. Over! His ID was discovered in his seat pocket. Over! The NYPD Dispatcher urges, "Stay in Place. Sending in the Paramedics. Over!" Dale Jacobs gets on his cell phone and dials Billy Black's number.

CHAPTER TWENTY-SIX

Inside Billy Black's moving vehicle, his cell phone rings. He answers.
"This is Billy Black!"
"Billy Black, this is Dale Jacobs NYPD."
"Officer Jacobs, how are things in the Big Apple?"
"You would not believe it if I told you."
"Hold on a minute, Officer Jacobs."
Billy Black merges his cell phone's audio with his radio. INTERCUTING between Billy Black in the

hunt for Abigail Creighton, Dale Jacobs of the NYPD, and The Pips also in the hunt for Abigail Creighton - hanging onto every word with varied emotions after that bridged call.
"What is happening, Officer? Talk to me. My Pips are all on the call. So, George Creighton confessed and turned himself in?"
 The other Pips are alerted and listen intently. "Worse... Upon the death of Noah Smith, we went over as you had asked us to secure the property along with non-recorded but existent evidence. Inside the master bedroom, we discovered George Creighton's body hanging from the roof by a noose."
Says Dale Jacobs.
"Really? What a way to die! Please preserve all footage and evidence."
Says Billy Black.
"You got it!"
Says Jacobs.
"Thanks for all you do. Please keep us posted on any other developments in the case. Will call you as soon as we catch her."
Says Billy Black.
Jacobs states with a swagger:
"We cannot wait!"

CHAPTER TWENTY-SEVEN

Billy Black, as well as the rest of The Pips, emotes.
"Do we have time for a pit stop?"
Asks Nichols.
"Warranted..!"
Injects, Redhead Girl.
The Pips take a quick pitstop and return to the hunt for the most wanted Abigail Creighton. Billy Black is hastened. He feels no holds barred.

"Time is of the essence. Our target, with that unprecedented head start, could be racing through Monaco with her eyes set on the Italian border. Activate all emergency protocols." As if pre-ordained, Monaco traffic gives The Pips the right-of-way. Meanwhile, Abigail Creighton entertains – catch me if you can.

Up ahead and out of The Pips' view. Abigail Creighton, driving the yellow speedster, is discombobulated. Tired of the stop-and-go traffic, she begins to dose off. Her vehicle swerves from lane to lane. Accidentally, her car almost rear-ends a crisp Mercedes Benz. She quickly regains her presence of mind.

"Darn! These people bought their licenses in Paris?" She says she will continue driving despite the mental lapses she encounters. She inadvertently almost rear-ends another automobile. She yawns and smacks both sides of her face with her right hand.
"Darn!"

A hotel sign for Columbus Monte-Carlo Hotel peaks. The exit ramp to it beckons. Her car exits. Moments later, she pulls into the small parking lot. Two Gen Z's, a BOY, and a GIRL approach. She rolls the passenger window down with a smile. Bonjour Madame!

The Girl greets. Bonjour.

Abigail Creighton responds. Vous parlez francais? The Girl says. What can I do for you? I am in desperate need of a nap.
States, Abigail Creighton. Her statement goes over their heads.
"Sleep!"
She reiterates.
"Okay. It would help if you had some sleep. Madame, we are college students and watch people's cars to buy textbooks. This is a crisp car; we will take care of no need to leave your keys. Upon checking out, just put some Euros in an envelope and leave them at the front desk. My name is Bill, and this is Carla." "Carla and Bill. It is a rental. This means any scratches it incurs, I will have to..."
Says Abigail Creighton.
"Madame, this is not our first rodeo. We will take extra care of your ride."
The Boy says with a smile. Abigail straggles towards the Front Desk.

CHAPTER TWENTY-EIGHT

Outside the Columbus Monte Hotel, Abigail checks for her car with the envelope marked with Carla and Bill in hand. Her car is missing. She scans the entire immediate area. Zip. Nada. Abigail immediately reaches for her iPhone and accesses the air tag Apps. "I cannot believe that I am getting acclimated to air tags. Hi Siri, where is my luggage?" The map on her phone points her to the local Chop Shop. "Chop Shop?" Abigail hustles on foot and drags her wheeled weekend bag. Scanning the area. She sees a worker outside transferring vehicle parts into a cube truck. At the same time, the sound of power tools alerts her to inside the Shop. Abigail darts inside the establishment. She sees her car on a lift and sees that its rear wheel is missing on the floor. The Car Chopper is busily fixed to dislodge the other rear wheel.

Abigail yells!

"Hey, this is my freaking car. What are you doing?"

He does not hear her. Lug nuts keep hitting the floor from his continued activity. Abigail steps into his space. Her two guns were drawn on him.

"This happens to be my ride. I want it out of here in less than ten minutes."

The ATTENDANT, seen packing the cube truck outside, walks in.

"Miss. Hold your horses. We have already paid the sellers for this vehicle. We owe you nothing."

"I do not ride horses. I'm not too fond of ropes. So, I'll keep holding my gun until I am forced to do so no longer."

She sways both guns in their direction.

"You now have less than eight minutes to put those wheels back on and approximately two minutes to release my car off your freaking lift. You feel me?"

The Attendant rushes to assist his co-worker assigned to the lift. In less than ten minutes, they push the car off the lift. Abigail throws her luggage in the trunk. The car door opens. Engine cuts on. Car motors off.

CHAPTER TWENTY-NINE

Billy Black's phone rings. He answers.
"This is Billy Black."
"Mr. Black. This is Chris Isaacs."
"Talk to me, Chris. What have you got?"
"Your target has just checked out from the Columbus Monte-Carlo Hotel, 23 Avenue Des Papalins. She rolled up in a car but left on foot."
"Intel interrupted, I guess. Do you have a picture of the car?"

"Yes. I have an updated one. It's on its way."
BLRING!
The phone rings. The image arrives on Billy Black's phone and Madison Allen's iPad. CU On Auto Image: A bright yellow Speedster. INTERCUTING between Billy Black and the other Pips. The auto image is received. Pips react positively to the news. Billy Black and The Pips pull up at Columbus Monte-Carlo Hotel. They survey the compound on foot in search of clues.

"I have a hunch this vehicle has left that location."
States Madison Allen. In the interim, The Redhead girl sees a white envelope on the ground. She grabs it. Bill & Carla are handwritten on it. Thanks. She opens it. Nothing is inside. The Attendant from the Chop Shop drives by and notices the seven automobiles parked in a cluster. He sees the seven motorists in a huddle. He intercedes.

Billy Black asks,

"Have you seen a yellow speedster come through lately?"

"She went East. She owes us money."

"For what?"

Billy Black asks. The Attendant shows a picture of the yellow car.

"She robbed us at gunpoint and took off." "How long ago was that?"

Asks Billy Black.
"Half an hour ago."
"Thanks. I hope she pays up."
Says, Billy Black.
"You chop?"
Asks, Ralph Gomez.
"Please don't hold it against me."
States, the Attendant. The Pips jump in their cars and head East. Billy Black's auto maintains the lead.

THE THUMB DRIVES

Copyright © 2024 by John A. Andrews

Books That Will Enhance Your Life

ISBN: 9798323081424

Cover Art: ALI

Cover Photo: ALI

All rights reserved.

THE THUMB DRIVES

FEATURING

THE PIPS

IN

MEDITERRANEAN PRIVATE EYE

SERIES

BY

JOHN ALAN ANDREWS

THE
THUMB DRIVES

TABLE OF CONTENTS

CHAPTER ONE...212
CHAPTER TWO...215
CHAPTER THREE...219
CHAPTER FOUR..223
CHAPTER FIVE..227
CHAPTER SIX...230
CHAPTER SEVEN...233
CHAPTER EIGHT...235
CHAPTER NINE..238
CHAPTER TEN...240
CHAPTER ELEVEN..243
CHAPTER TWELVE..246
CHAPTER THIRTEEN..249
CHAPTER FOURTEEN..252
CHAPTER FIFTEEN...255
CHAPTER SIXTEEN...257
CHAPTER SEVENTEEN...261
CHAPTER EIGHTEEN..264
CHAPTER NINETEEN..267
CHAPTER TWENTY..270
CHAPTER TWENTY-ONE..272

CHAPTER ONE

A DRONE SHOT of Grasse, a northern city in Southern France, reveals its multi-faceted landscape, adorned with rolling hills, valleys, plateaus, and expansive shorelines. Nestled in its geography, commercial and residential abode, pops.

A medium shot of a man's backside takes center stage. He is medium built, in the 50s, dressed in a black hoody, and faces the sunset with his hind end turned opposite the nightfall.

He remains stationary like a manikin. Even so, he does not show his face. Droning beyond his existence are ancient village valleys, highlighting edifices set in ancient architecture, and sparse, slow-moving vehicular traffic juxtaposes.

A house looms adjacent to the steepled church. The Vibe is eerie and evil. The window curtains accommodate daylight fluttering in the gentle breeze.

Wishing for clarity, push inside the living room. A silhouette traverses. Subsequently, laser focus on the left, a black-haired Maria Charles in her 50s moving forward, fosters a penetrative look and lingers for a beat. Lingering smog obscures her right eye and half-face.

Fully open-mouthed, she blows the smog away before disappearing briskly into oblivion.

The fully open-mouthed Maria gently blows the smog away and briskly disappears into oblivion.

A beat. She returns, now with snow-white hair. Plus, tears of blood mar her face.

Focused, she stares into the eyes of eight-year-old Melissa Daniel. Her left hand is in a black glove, and she points directly at Melissa using her curved index finger.

Melissa remains poised, reading from a sacred book held with both hands. She cradles the book without battening an eye. Then, it blinks once.

Maria's face comes into focus, overpowering and overshadowing a portion of the prayer book.

Melissa sees Maria as an evil witch who meets her fate - shot to death.

Maria sees Melissa as a decomposed doll residing in the bushes.

CHAPTER TWO

A man neatly dressed in a business suit rotates the Plexi glass sign FOLLOW ME in his hand with the other hand. While intermittently toying with his cell phone. His face is oblivious. Troubled Villagers wait in earnest. The Big Red does not return, and neither does Melissa. It is a tear-shed environment. Meanwhile, Traffic builds up in that small community and gridlock.

Tension mounts as the search for Melissa cascades. Foot traffic is also at an all-time high. Emerging on foot from that traffic buildup, her Mom, ESTHER DANIEL, in her late 40s, is teary-eyed and pounces. She is the split image of her daughter.

Her sighing escalates to balling, and she plunges into total disarray. Regaining her presence of mind, she musters some gravitas and distributes her phone number on slips of paper to the angry, mourning crowd.

Drying her eyes,

"I knew she had an affinity for cars, exotic cars. I never knew she would take it so far. She was only eight years old. She is still a child. What was that driver thinking? Someone, please help!"

The Villagers, grief-stricken, indulge, console, and empathize. Some are busily working on their phones.

One VILLAGER, in particular, traverses the sidewalk with the cell phone up against her ear.

"Someone has to have seen little Melissa. No one captured that car's license tag?"

No one affirms.

The Villages press on in mental saw cloth and ashes.

Mobile Police presence builds instantly. It is a K-9 dog hullabaloo.

RADIO TRANSMITS.

RADIO STATIC LINGERS.

RADIO STATIC CLEARS.

An alert French Police Officer, MIKE ROGERS, leading his K-9, responds,

"This is Lieutenant Mike Rogers. Go ahead."

INTERCUTTING between his Captain MARK CROISIRE smoking a cigarette and Mike Rogers.

Captain Mark Croisire responds,

"Mike, we have more trouble on our hands. Another Hitch Hiker is reported missing in the North. We need to get some of your guys up North ASAP."

"Is there anything else we need to know?"

Asks Mike Rogers.

"That is all we know at this moment. BTW, tell Miss Daniel I feel her pain; my twin girls are Melissa's age."

Says Captain Mark Croisire.

"What is the split, Captain?"

Asks Mike Rogers.

"Mike, I would say do fifty-fifty until we can get some of our reserves in."

"You got it, Captain."

Mike Rogers surveys and alternately speaks on his radio.

"Grassley, Charles, Benoit, Franklin, Peters, Moss, Haversham, Michaels, Schumer, and Sagamore, head North!"

Those Police Officers mentioned races back to their Cruisers. They return K-9s to the kennel on the rear seat and jump in on the front seat. They buckle up. Their cruisers motor off.
FLASHING EMERGENCY LIGHTS
SIRENS CRESCENDO.

CHAPTER THREE

One day earlier, A Model type figure, Naomi Charles, using a cardboard sign, dressed in a sexy two-piece, dark sunglasses, and dancing sensually while she thumbed a ride. The French Police have been made aware.
Investigator Sagamore surveys the streets.
RADIO STATIC
RADIO STATIC CLEARS

CAPTAIN MARK CROISIRE

"A twenty-year-old Naomi Charles has been unaccounted for since yesterday. It is alleged a motorist picked her up, and she has not been heard from since. We need every officer on this intense search."

Those eleven dispatched Police Officers in cruisers briskly join the regional hunt.

LOCALS parade with signs bearing the name Naomi Charles. You Are Not Forgotten!

The demonstration progresses as it grows. People from all social classes, mixed in with the LOCALS, are in attendance—it's rowdy.

The Locals chant:

Bring our Naomi back to us! Bring our Naomi back to us!

A gifted SINGER in the crowd craves center stage and erupts.

Bring back. Bring back. Bring back Naomi to us today. (Reprise)

At the intersection, Captain Mark Croisire steps up to the podium.

"This is indeed a hard act to follow. You do mourn deeply."

He gets teary-eyed but continues,

"It has been a horrendous Seventy-two hours. Two of our local girls are now missing. Missing without a trace is never a good sign in the police business."
He takes in the mourners.
"Mr. And Mrs. Charles, we'll find out the underlying cause of these disappearances and bring whoever is doing this to justice. Our community would not accept less of us. Naomi and Melissa deserve to be present. My officers are already in the field, working on these two cases. Investigator Welch will head up the investigation moving forward. Welch, the ball is now in your court."
Welch smiles broadly in self-approval.
INVESTIGATOR WELCH off-microphone:
"Remember, to rein in your little ones and even those not so little."
The gathering applauds willy-nilly.
The Locals chant:
Bring Naomi back to us, along with Melissa. We need a kibosh, a kibosh!
Captain Croisire steps away from the pulpit.
Naomi's mother, PHYLLIS CHARLES, and her dad, GRAFTON CHARLES, immediately fill his place and brace the microphonic podium.
Chants and applauses mount from the Locals.
We are with you. We want justice!
Phyllis Charles presides,

"Thank you. We need everyone's help in this search. Naomi was a good girl. She was. She turns 21 tomorrow. This should not have been her fate. It is now forty-four hours and counting.
Grafton Charles states,
"Let us also not forget. That 8-year-old girl from the south, Melissa, is also missing. It is a strong possibility they may never find her. Somebody needs to do something and find the villains behind this."
A WOMAN in the crowd holding up a big SAVE NAOMI! Cardboard signs and yells:
"We not only need more street lights, but we need more street cameras, more on-the-beat Cops, and candid neighborhood watch!"
Grafton Charles from within the crowd,
"We sure do. Our Mayor is not here..."
Captain Mark Croisire interjects,
"He got stuck in a meeting."
The Locals, saving face, in chorus ask,
"He is fighting off the Yellow Jackets?"
Later. The crowd thins out.

CHAPTER FOUR

Officer Sagamore notices a brown object ahead on the green grass from his moving cruiser. His cruiser immediately pulls over curbside. He investigates. It is the ANYWHERE cardboard sign that Naomi once displayed while hitching a ride.
Sagamore pulls his vehicle to the shoulder of the road, secures the evidence inside the trunk of his cruiser, and continues his search deep into the streets of the woods.

Suddenly, he notices a bloodied corpse on the shoulder of the road. Flies saturate the remains. He investigates and discovers the mutilated body of a woman. It fits the description of Naomi Charles. On her person, he retrieves her Driver's License. In his preview, it is added up.
He radios.
RADIO STATIC DOMINATES
He tries again.
RADIO STATIC DISSIPATES
INTERCUTING between Officer Sagamore and the fuming Captain Mark Croisire.
"Come in. This is Captain Croisire."
"This is Officer Sagamore."
"Where the heck are you, Sagamore? Your colleagues have been trying to find you. Welch is having a heart attack. No radio? We cannot afford these glitches during a Mayoral campaign."
"Sorry, it operates like a teetertotter. Sometimes it does, sometimes it doesn't."
"Well, trade that darn radio in for one that works!"
Officer Sagamore assimilates the instruction,
"FYI, I came upon a body in the woods. It could be that Hiker, Naomi. You know, the Hitchhiker who was carrying the ANYWHERE sign. I recovered that sign a few yards away. It looks like someone took an axe to her."

"An axe? Sagamore, be careful insinuating evidence you cannot prove."
"It sure looks like an axe was used, Captain."
Says Sagamore.
Captain Mark Croisire cannot believe what he is hearing.
"Keep an eye on that body. We are sending in the paramedics and their entire department."
He says.
Officer Sagamore tries to convince his Captain,
"Yes, Sir!"
Sagamore returns to his car and waits. From his cruiser, flashing emergency lights illuminate.
The other assigned ten police cruisers bear down, accompanied by other emergency vehicles.
Paramedics, Investigators, and Coroners jump out.
Officer Sagamore, stepping out of his car, greets. He points to the mutilated corpse.
They investigated and retrieved a pair of sunglasses as evidence. Plus, Naomi Charles once wore that pair of boots.
The body is placed inside a body bag and wheeled into a Paramedic's vehicle.
Sagamore follows, the focused Investigator Welch walking away from the scene.
Officer Sagamore's curiosity peaks,
"What do we know, anything?"

Investigator Welch states,
"Nothing yet."
While staring at the pathologists boarding a vehicle.
"We'll have to wait and see."
He continues.
Sagamore wants more. Nothing. Zilch.
He notices another Investigator leaving the scene.
"What is all the waiting for?"
He asks.
The Investigator responds,
"We need to turn these cases over to..."
"Welch? Why?"
Asks, Sagamore.
Sagamore, I only do as I'm instructed.
The Investigator responds.
Sagamore waits for the next shoe to drop. It does not fall. The Investigator boards his automobile and drives away.

CHAPTER FIVE

Naomi's parents and other villagers are in mourning at the candlelight visual. Flowers and lit candles decorate the scene. It is a dragged-out somber event. On the periphery, the empathic Officer Sagamore keeps community watch seated inside his cruiser.

In the interim, news spread amongst mourners that MEREDITH SHU, an Asian woman in her 20s descending the mountain slopes, dovetailed a hike and met HARVEY LOPEZ, a Caucasian man in his

40s, coming up more than two weeks ago. He was mainly geared for a climb.
"How were the slopes treacherous?"
He asked Meridith, sipping from her water bottle.
"Not bad. I have climbed more definitely. Maybe Mt. Everest is next,
She states.
"I am new to this. Never know what to expect."
He responds.
"New to these slopes or hiking?"
"Both."
Says Harvey, looking down at his half-tied shoelaces. He continues,
"Can't you tell? We don't have these slopes in Cannes. Just miles and miles of hotels, restaurants, and docks."
"Yep. Been there. The rich and famous lunge. However, nothing beats a prepared mind when it comes to hiking. You may want to start with properly tied shoestrings."
Says Meridith Shu.
"Thanks for being so observant."
Says Harvey, securing his shoestring and getting set for the ascent.
"I live a mile down the hill at the Flats. Reach out if you need some hiking tips."
Meredith says.

"I am Harvey Lopez..."
"I am Meredith Shu..."
They take out their cell phones and exchange numbers.
"Enjoy the slopes, Harvey."
"Safe travel, Meredith."
They depart contrariwise. Meredith is delighted.

CHAPTER SIX

One week ago, Harvey and Meredith walked hand in hand. They are laughing and joking, looking like they belong together along the streets of Grasse.
Subsequently, Meredith embarks on an investigative undertaking. She arrives at Nice Airport.
Harvey Lopez's car pulls away from the curb. Inside: A strange Woman occupies the front passenger seat. Meredith's car trails Harvey's, which stops at a Lounge in Cannes. Meredith, disguised trails on foot.

Harvey and the woman enter the longue and camp on a lobby couch.

Meredith gets a bird' s-eye view of Harvey Lopez caressing the Woman's body. She basks in his TLC.

Oblivious to Harvey and the Woman, Meredith is on site and expands her investigation. She pounces, cell phone ready. She sneaks up and covertly captures the romantic rendezvous.

Too hard to manage, Meredith tears up after the last capture.

Later. Meredith calls Harvey from her hotel room.

INTERCUTTING between Meredith and Harvey Lopez in his parked car.

Meredith, ailing:

"How could you do that to me?"

"Do what? What are you talking about?"

Asks Harvey.

"With that woman. You are such a freaking cheat!"

"What are you talking about?"

Asks Harvey.

"Talking about? I have the video. Want to see?"

She asks.

"You took a video of me and some girl. You B...! What if it was my sister?"

"Don't talk to me that way. Besides, do you do that to your sister? Are you a freaking inbreeding monster?"

"Why don't you bring the video over to the crib? So, can we watch it together? You are trying to be a rich Asian Woman. That is so against the grain."

"No. I will choose none of the above. I will save it for when she does the same thing to you. I should have known. It is a good thing I didn't give it up... My mother taught me well. Never give it up on the first date."

SILENCE

Harvey aborts the call.

Meredith stares into the phone.

"You monster! Heart breaker!

Harvey doesn't buy into her belittlement of him. He yells,

Dissipater! Have an excellent life!"

CHAPTER SEVEN

Meredith traverses the shoreline as the sun begins to set. She is not in high spirits as when she first met Harvey Lopez. Depressed, the dispirited Meredith departs towards the village.

Meredith arrived outside her house, still. She was drying her tears when she noticed an object on her car windscreen hitched between the wipers.

She investigates. It is a long-stemmed red rose with a note attached: I am Sorry - Meredith! She is not impressed.

"You should have watched that Western movie – Unforgiven.

Ignoring the pleasantry and enragement, she kicks all four tires on her car and then systematically punctures them by disengaging the valves on each. An elderly female Observer notices as the car fully reclines onto its four rims. She looks for the perpetrator and sees no one.

Meanwhile, Meredith enters the house unnoticed by the onlooker. Inside, she accesses her computer and posts Harvey and the Woman's romantic interlude on Instagram. In less than an hour, it goes viral.

Meredith has had enough and endeavors to get away from it all. Have an excellent life, Harvey – she internalizes.

Meredith hits the streets in hitch-and-hike mode, backpack-laden and holding up a large cardboard sign: MARRY ME, PLEASE.

Even so, she looks confused, one of deep betrayal. Subsequently, Meredith disappears off the radar.

CHAPTER EIGHT

Billy Black traverses the city of Nice, seeking to solve the case of these disappearing hitchhikers. The car radio is on, and he listens to some Hip-Hop music.
A RADIO ANNOUNCER interrupts:
"We interrupt to bring you some breaking news. A third Hitch Hiker has disappeared in the city of Grasse. An Asian woman, Meredith

Shu has disappeared within the last 24 hours. This now brings the total to three within the previous week. So far, the mutilated corpse of Naomi Charles has been recovered.

However, the 8-year-old Melissa and Daniel are still missing.

Additionally, Officer Sagamore, one of the lead investigators on the Hitch Hiker's trail, is missing. He was instrumental in finding the recently slain hitchhiker, Naomi Charles. Could Officer Sagamores' disappearance be related to friendly sabotage? A question now asked by many law enforcement agencies in the French Riviera."

Billy Black digests the news.

"When it rains, it pours buckets."

He says.

A few beats. He dials.

INTERCUTTING between Billy Black and Investigator Welch at his house watching TV while drinking a Kro 66 beer and Billy Black on the phone.

"Investigator Welch, this is Billy Black."

"Mr. Black, how are you and those Pips doing? Keeping your noses clean?"

"We are doing great and keeping a lid on crime. You and your team could use some help in the city of Grasse. The word is out: You are losing your men. Plus, the citizens, both women and young girls."

"I have heard on the streets that you are fixing to take over this investigation, Black."

It does not yet have our biometrics. This is my initial conversation with you concerning this investigation. Welch, it bothers me when men in uniform disappear randomly, without a trace."

"Yep. It looks like we lost Sagamore."

Welch takes a swig of his beer.

"Black. News spread quickly in France. If you are cooking onions, close the kitchen windows."

"Not sure where you are getting your news."

"I'm listening so keenly, Black – I can hear a whisper."

CHAPTER NINE

Billy black maintains that serious look on his face—Welch clues in.

"Well. Under the radar, you must have heard that we now have territorial access to the entire Mediterranean, every country, and every city."

"What will you do that we haven't done, Black?"

"Stop the bleeding, Welch. Stop the bleeding. How many more people will have to die before some real investigators descend upon the city of Grasse?"

"What makes you think you will become a force to be reckoned with across the Mediterranean? "
Billy Black isn't feeling him.
"There are too many languages unless you reshuffle and create a team of linguists."
"Time. All we need is time, Welch."
Welch is furious. He feels underrated. He stares at the Mediterranean map on his living room wall. He feels hot under the collar. He turns off the TV and paces.
"Grasse? Eventually, they will have to learn not to put themselves in harm's way. Sitting on a hot stove would not make it any cooler.
"Not sure that Officer Sagamore, one of your guys, put himself in harm's way. It seems he was just doing his job, Welch, lifting victims off the hot stove."
There is an incoming call on Billy Black's phone. It IDs SMOOTH JOE.
Billy Black states:
"Welch, Police Business is what we do. Got to go. Best of luck."

CHAPTER TEN

INTERCUTING between Billy Black and Smooth Joe while Smooth Joe is having a beer at Le Majestic Hotel.
"Smooth Joe, what's happening in Cannes?"
The waitress excuses herself and lowers the music. Smooth Joe responds,
"I don't like being left hung out to dry. Ever since our last rendezvous with Noah and

Abigail Creighton, according to Otis Redding,

"I feel like I have been sitting on the dock of a bay, watching the tide roll away. "I am all about Sam Cooke and the Chain Gang. That's the sound of the men…"

Smooth Joe changing the conversation:

"I heard there is work in Grasse.

Accordingly, it could be more than The Pips can manage. Yes?"

"Really? You are underestimating us, Smooth Joe."

"What's going on with my resume, Black?"

"I have mentioned before that I do not work in human resources, and the last I heard, you were still on probation and not allowed to carry a firearm. Those are the naked facts, Smooth Joe. Those are the facts."

"Your guys are keeping me differently abled, Black."

"You will always be an ally, Smooth Joe. I will link up in Cannes."

"I don't want to wait in vain for this gig. Even so, I'll be here at Le Majestic. Want to hear more about that expansive move in the Mediterranean."

"Kool. First, the city of Grasse is on our list."

Billy Black dials Al Nobles.

INTERCUTTING between Billy Black and Al Nobles as Al surfs the Web on his CPU.

Al Nobles takes the call.

"Nobles. Too much is going on in Grasse. We need to put our tentacles in that city.
"I can be there in two hours, Black. Count me in."
BILLY BLACK declares,
"Reinforcement will arrive within 24 hours!"

CHAPTER ELEVEN

Later. Al Nobles recovers fragments of hitchhiker Meredith Shu's backpack. It is soaked with blood.

Her cell phone, her laptop, pair of sunglasses, and white headphones, along with the folded blood-stained sign MARRY ME PLEASE, are also recovered at the crime scene.

The mutilated corpse gets placed in a body bag and removed from the scene. Al Nobles continues to investigate the crime scene.

Back on the road and inside Billy Black's car, his 9-year-old DAMIEN BLACK gazing at the morning traffic. He looks across at his Dad.

"Dad, with all these Hitch Hikers dropping like flies, what are the odds: You, possibly posing as a Hitch Hiker? You have the black belt, the brown belt, and even the purple belt. You go in and clean up the chaos. I know that no one messes with you. You will take it to them. Won't you, Dad?"

"Thanks, Damien."

"That would be brilliant! Right, Dad. What do you think?"

"I thought you understood that I don't discuss police business with family members."

"Not even probabilities? What if it involved a member of the family or one of your partners?"

"Were you eavesdropping on my conversation last night?"

"No, Dad. I went straight to sleep with school on my mind. However, I heard you said Redhead Girl could replicate a Hitch Hiker. Also, I said my prayers."

"So, you have been eavesdropping?"

"Partly. I am not going to be grounded, right, Dad? Poor Melissa. All she needed was a ride on her birthday."

The car pulls up outside the school.

"Have a great day, Dad."
They high-five".
"Have a great day, DB. Your Mom will pick you up. Remember, Police business is Police business and confidential department information."
"Mom. She drives with both hands on the steering wheel and steps on the brakes around corners. Could The Pips get her a siren, Dad?"
"She believes in safe driving…and doesn't wear a badge."
Damien opens the car door and exits.
"Okay, Dad!"
The School Guard steps up and escorts Damien into the building.
Billy Black drives away.

CHAPTER TWELVE

Outside The Pips Headquarters, Billy Black's auto pulls up and parks. He gets out and hustles inside. Redhead Girl is dressed in shorts, a tank top, sneakers, sunglasses, and a backpack. Hugs from the rest of the Pips are in order.
"Phelps, Do you have everything you need?"
"Yep."
Madison Allen looks Phelps over and sheds a tear.

"Don't cry for me... Madison. I have signed up for this, remember? It is all or nothing with The Pips!"
Billy Black eyes the other five members of his team.
Billy Black to Al Nobles:
"Al Nobles, drop Phelps off in Grasse."
Al Nobles smiles; he is up to the task.

Redhead Girl boards Al's car.

ENGINE CUTS ON

DOORS SLAM

CAR ROARS OFF

Meanwhile, on the road in Northern Grasse, two Gen Z students, Daisy Croft and Alex Charles, are thumbing a ride on a desolate roadway. They are backpack-strapped, wearing shorts and sunglasses.

Later. Al Nobles arrives in Northern Grasse. The grounds are bloody. He recovers backpacks, sunglasses, and the bodies of Daisy Croft and Alex Charles, mutilated on the side of the road. Blood residue lingers on the ground, along with a large knife saturated with blood.

Billy Black's phone rings inside his moving automobile.

INTERCUTTING between Billy Black, Al Nobles in the driver's seat, and Redhead Girl on her cell phone.

Hello Al. How is Redhead Girl? How is the hunt?
Redhead Girl answers:
"Bloody! Out the gate. We have discovered the bodies of two students brutally murdered and along at the scene, most likely the weapon of choice."
"So, you are in the neck of their woods?"
"Yep. Al, I've got an investigative hunch. Could you drop me off here?"
Billy Black ponders.
Al Nobles drives over to the curb.
Redhead Girl gets out of the car, backpack-laden.
"Do you still want to proceed with this?"
Asks Billy Black.
"I have this!"
Says Redhead Girl.
Al Nobles, overhearing the conversation, stares at Redhead Girl with empathy.
"One must do what one must do. I'll cover the crime scene."
She says.
"Sounds good, Al. Phelps, I'll be trailing you."
Says Billy Black.
"Sounds good. I'm thrilled to be standing in the gap."
Responds Redhead Girl as she boards Al Noble's vehicle.

CHAPTER THIRTEEN

Inside Billy Black's automobile, the radio is on. Hip Hop Music plays.
RADIO ANNOUNCER
A gunman entered the Nice Middle School at least an hour ago. There has been no report of casualty. However, the school is in lockdown amid this brewing investigation.

Billy Black grasps tightly onto the steering wheel. His car makes a U-turn and heads back toward the school in question. He accesses his phone and immediately calls the school. He gets a busy signal, and his car speeds up.

Minutes later, he arrives at the school amid massive traffic congestion and a deluge of cold sweat.

The wailing of parents and guardians greets, some in wonderment, as the school goes on lockdown and is heavily guarded by security personnel.

Additional Law enforcement personnel traverse. Police cruisers bear down. The milieu is a twisted state of confusion.

Billy Black exits his car and joins the line of parents and guardians waiting to get their kids.

Billy Black sees a busy male School Attendant, sweating. Before he can utter a word, the School Attendant says,

"Mr. Black, it will take at least an hour for parents to pick up their kids. We are indeed sorry about the inconvenience and the situation at hand."

Billy Black breathing familiarity for the attendant,

"Is Damien okay?"

"Damien, your son is. He is a hero."

Billy black waits for the next shoe to fall conversationally. It does not.

Billy Black is antsy.

"A Hero? Sir! What do you mean?"

The School Attendant briskly returns inside amid static on his handheld radio.

Billy Black, cemented in a state of confusion, misses a phone call from Phelps. Regaining his presence of mind, he redials Phelps. Traffic bottlenecks and gridlock supervene.

Phelps is on the phone.

"Phelps, it is going to take a bit longer. There has been a gunman incident at my son's school, and the info remains sketchy.

INTERCUTTING between Phelp's mobile in Al Noble's automobile and Billy Black's parked automobile outside the school compound.

"Is he OK?"

Asks Phelps.

The call drops.

CHAPTER FOURTEEN

Corie Phelps redials.

"Sorry, I guess I hit a dead spot. So, is Damien okay?"

"He should be according to the information obtained from the School Attendant. He said something about Damien being a hero without any footnotes. This remains sketchy.

ABOUT AN HOUR EARLIER: Damien was in his classroom with three other students of various ethnicities. They were engaged in their schoolwork.
EMERGENCY ALARM SOUNDS
An ACTIVATED LOUD SPEAKER SYSTEM crescendo. "Gunman on the premises! Hunker down!"
Damien abandons his class and darts to the closed-circuit TV room. He opens and closes the door behind him.
Damien focuses on the close-circuit monitors.
He sees the gunman gunning up the stairs close to where he resides. Damien gets down on all fours and engages in pushups. Peripherally, he eyes the broom in the corner. The gap under the door summons.
Damien grabs the broom. While watching the TV monitors, he strides towards the door and sees the silhouette of the Gunman ascending towards the door.
He methodically sticks the broomstick under the door. The Gunman trips over the broomstick, falls flat on his face, and loses his hold of his assault weapon.
Multiple Security personnel descend on the Gunman's trail like a swarm of bees to honey. They trap him, buttonhole, and restrain him before he can

get up and retrieve his assault weapon off the floor. He breaks loose and becomes confrontational. They struggle to restrain him. The gun is now in his grasp. They wrestle his weapon away and administer handcuffs.

One Security Officer picks up the broom and lodges it inside the closed-circuit TV Room. He sees movements under the table and draws his weapon, ready to shoot. Before popping off a round at the suspect, he notices that Damien Black is under the table.

He yells:

"Come on out of there, little fellow. We've caught him. Thanks for your bravery. However, stay out of harm's way next time and leave it up to the professionals."

Damien stares at him, concerned.

"You've caught him, right?"

"We did! You could have gotten hurt.

The Security Officer leads Damien out of the room.

CHAPTER FIFTEEN

Back to the present. Billy Black waits in his car outside his son's school. His phone rings.
"Billy Black!"
He answers.
Redhead Girl is on the phone.
"It is slow out here. Not one vehicle passed this way in the last fifteen minutes. You picked up your son, right?"

"We are poised to move in soon. They are now allowing parents to pick up their kids. Here he comes. Phelps, are you sure you are ready to do this?"

"Mr. Black, that's what I've signed up for, right?"

"I've got your back."

Billy Black hangs up as Damien boards the car, giving him High-fives.

Damien celebrates.

"I did it, Dad. I stopped Gunman. When can I join The Pips!"

"Since when did they begin arming kids at school?" Asked Billy Black.

"The broomstick. No bullets necessary when you know how to disarm the suspect."

"What if the broomstick missed?"

"It did not, Dad. I caught the sucker. You can ask Principal Jones."

"You are perpetually trying to play cop. Please leave it to those who carry a shield and a weapon. Will you?"

"Grounded, Dad?"

"Yep. Grounded. Playing cop could get you killed. I heard the shooter was carrying an assault weapon, Damien."

"He did, Dad."

CHAPTER SIXTEEN

The frustrated Redhead Girl waits, backpacking, saddled on a side street in Grasse. A car rolls up with a male DRIVER in his 30s. The Redhead Girl thumbs. It stops. She scouts in.
"Thanks. Thank you so much!"
He looks bright but strange.
"How long has it been since you were thumbing a drive?"
He asks.

"More than an hour. I recall. I am so thankful for the lift. I mean the ride."
"You are welcome. I am glad I can be of service. You are different. Most hitchhikers I have picked over the years are not very appreciative. It is all about them getting where they want to go. Take them exactly where they want to go. What is your destination, College Student?"
Redhead Girl replies,
"Grasse. North Grasse."
"You don't have an exact address?"
"Just drop me off at a safe place in North Grasse, and I can figure out the rest."
The Driver smiles,
"You are an Explorer, aren't you?"
"Why? Why do you think so?"
Answers Redhead Girl.
"Are you?"
He asks.
"It is in my pedigree."
Says Redhead Girl.
"Yep. That backpack. It looks laden."
Says the Driver with a sublimed smile.
"Just a facade. I hate school but like the study of rocks."
"Geologist?"
Redhead Girl shakes her head YES.

The car wipers are swishing lightly as it begins to snow.

The Driver continues:

"I hate school. Plus, I haven't read a book since leaving high school. No need to."

Redhead Girl ponders,

"Most people have not, either. So, you pick up hitchhikers out of the kindness of your heart?"

They pass a Blonde thumbing a ride in the rain. The driver looks the other way and asks:

"Why is your leading legal question? I picked you up. Didn't I?"

"Yes, and I thank you for your generosity."

The Driver continues,

"Off that lonely highway."

The car swerves to the left and then to the right.

Redhead Girl is rattled,

"Ouch! Bald tires?"

SILENCE

The car swerves again. This time from right to left.

Redhead Girl continues,

"What the heck are you doing?"

"Driving. Why are you asking questions for which you already know the answer?"

Redhead Girl responds hysterically:

"Will you please stop and let me out? We have arrived in North Grasse. I'll find my way from here."

"You've got to be kidding me? In this wilderness?"
The car swerves again from left to right.
Redhead Girl is agitated:
"Yes. I will walk to the rest of my destination. I cannot stand Maniacs."
"I thought you said you had already arrived at North Grasse. Did your GPS inside your backpack malfunction?"

CHAPTER SEVENTEEN

The beeping sound emits and continues from Redhead Girl's backpack.
The Driver is alarmed.
Redhead Girl cracks open the door.
The car swerves again as the car races through a desolate community.
The car swerves again.

An embankment beckons.

The redhead girl grabs the steering wheel away from the driver.

The Driver attempts to control the car's trajectory in vain.

The car careens into the dam on the passenger side.

ENGINE IS RUNNING IDLY

The struggle for steering wheel control to land a rebound is futile.

Redhead Girl lands a punch in the Driver's face. Flush.

The Driver winches and comes back at her with an uppercut. She defends it tactfully and lands a punch close to the Driver's jugular.

A tooting Tractor Trailer bears down on the narrow strip.

Redhead Girl reaches inside her backpack and retrieves her gun.

The Driver darts out through the driver's door and speeds off on foot.

In a split second. Already in the driver's seat, Redhead Girl steers the car in alignment with the street, allowing the eighteen-wheeler to pass quickly.

Redhead Girl puts her gun on the passenger seat and her backpack on the car's floor. She drives off in exploration mode, looking across at the gun on the seat. Redhead Girl says under her breath:

"Why did I not use you on him? Delayed intelligence is every investigator's nightmare."

She adjusts the rearview mirror.

The Driver does not pursue her.

She buoys up and empties the glove compartment. She throws the finds onto the passenger seat. The picture of a white run-down house peaks. She continues driving. Up ahead. A white, run-down house in the distance pops.

Fact-finding. Redhead Girl drives towards it. She pulls into the driveway.

Pressed up against the window pane, a little girl gets her attention.

As the car nears the house, the girl's unkempt condition becomes more apparent.

Redhead Girl waves. The girl reciprocates.

With both hands over the mouth in the shape of a funnel.

CHAPTER EIGHTEEN

Redhead Girl stares deep into the little Girl's soul, whose clothes are tattered and hair unkempt.
"What is your name?"
She asks.
The Girl responds,
"Melissa. I am eight years old. This is a caricature."
"Melissa. Are you home alone?"
Asks Redhead Girl.
"Yes. The others are feared dead.

"Can I come in?"
Asks Redhead Girl.
Redhead Girl moves closer to gaining entrance.
"The door is locked. Maria has the key. She is out looking for more Hitch Hikers."
Says Melissa
"Okay. Little Girl. Please do not get close to that door. It could be wired. Is it?"
"It is not hot."
"Back up!"
Says Redhead Girl as she kicks the door in.
Melissa cheers in amazement, aided by loud applause. Redhead Girl enters.
"It stinks in here. Redhead Girl covers her nostrils with her hand."
"It has been as if I moved here the second day.
"My name is Phelps. You can call me Corie. They also call me Redhead Girl. We must get you out of here immediately."
"I don't think so. You can get in but not get out of here."
Says Melissa.
On the wall, inscribed in blood, THE THUMB DRIVES.
Melissa takes stock of the sign and ponders.
Maria would be upset if you took me away. My job is to watch the house."

"Really?"

Asks Redhead Girl as she steals detailed looks within the house.

"Who is Maria? "

Asks Redhead Girl.

"She must have driven you here like she did me."

"No. She did not. I found my way to you after punching daylights out of this guy. I've got this! I will be right back."

Redhead Girl darts outside to the car. She pops open the trunk. Inside: A bloody axe, giant-sized rain boots, multiple wigs - colored white, coveralls, multiple cell phones, and backpacks.

CHAPTER NINETEEN

Redhead Girl returns to the house in a mad rush.
"You must be a Cop. You don't leave any stone unturned."
Says Melissa.
"Yep. An Investigator. We must get out of here promptly.
"What about those Hitchhikers in the basement?"
Asks Redhead Girl.
Melissa ponders and responds to her in tears,

"How many?"

"Yes. How many?"

Redhead Girl demands the answer after Melissa regains her presence of mind.

"I have lost count. More than all my fingers and toes. They checked in but never checked out."

Redhead Girl takes the initiative and takes a peek into the basement.

"Follow me!"

She sees multiple body parts, along with a slew of corpses.

A RADIO TRANSMITS

Redhead Girl attends to the transmitting gadget inside her backpack as she reverses from down the stairs. With one hand squeezing her nostrils, she facilitates the radio transmission.

RADIO (O.S.) We have got you on GPS. We are coming in.

Billy Black's voice echoes.

"Thanks, Billy Black."

Says The Redhead Girl.

The sound of moving vehicles saturates the White House's interior.

Six Pips' cruisers bear down on the White House yard. Multiple emergency vehicles accompany the law enforcement convoy. Melissa and Redhead Girl abandon their current activities. Melissa gravitates and looks through the window pane. Redhead Girl peers through the front door.

CHAPTER TWENTY

Billy Black, Madison Allen, Yovanda Nichols, Vince Taylor, Ralph Gomez, and Al Nobles exit their vehicles and enter the house, armed.

Madison Allen grabs Melissa and brings her to the front door. Melissa clutches tightly to a small black purse.

Taking no chances, Madison Allen takes the purse and hands it to Yovanda Nichols.

"This belongs to Melissa. Please give it to her at the end of the trip."

Madison surveys as two accompanied Paramedics escort Melissa to their vehicle. The emergency transport motors are off.

Meanwhile, a Tow Truck lifts the parked Driver's car and tows it away.

Inside the house. Coroners, Pathologists, and other Paramedics enter the house in droves. They filter to the basement with body bags. It is a grotesque milieu.

Reacting to the rancidness, they examine the carnage, collect mountains of evidence, and accommodate with body bags.

On the outside. The Pips depart, roaming the neighborhood in six vehicles. Redhead Girl rides with Billy Black.

They survey the entire neighborhood. There's nothing to see regarding their case; they cool their heels.

CHAPTER TWENTY-ONE

Out of their view, a tow truck bears down, zooming past the paramedic's vehicle. It swings in front of that emergency vehicle and immediately slows its roll. This series of vehicular tantrums aggravates the two Paramedics in the front seats.

From inside the rear section of the vehicle, Melissa yells:

"Help! Help! That is her car!"
The driver of the Paramedics' vehicle hears her.
"What are you doing, man? How about staying in your lane?"
 Asked the driver, who serves the paramedic vehicle towards the tow truck in retaliation.
The Tow Truck drops the Driver's vehicle, releases its additional grasp on it, and takes off speedily.
The Paramedic vehicle is trapped as it avoids a collision with the tow truck and the Driver's car. The Paramedic vehicle driver discombobulated – radios. The gadget is inundated with static.
The Driver jumps out and saunters toward the driver's side of the Paramedic Vehicle.
Melissa yells:
"That's her. That's her car. I know it! Watch out. She will kill you, too."
Melissa is animated and grabs the attention of the lone Female Paramedic lounging in the rear of the vehicle.
In the interim, the Paramedic from inside the vehicle jumps out in attack mode toward the Driver, who is now exiting the car. The Paramedic vehicle's rear door is left ajar.
Melissa reaches for the little black purse where the female paramedic sat and opens it.

Inside is a Radio. She is ecstatic about the find. Quickly, she searches for the call button and radios.

"We are under attack!"

The Driver is out of the car and moves to the front of the vehicle while warding off the female paramedic. The Paramedic Vehicle driver gets slashed by the Driver. He falls to the ground.

Mellisa over the Radio:

"She just killed the driver of the Ambulance. Now, she is going after the other guy."

The Pips intercept.

The other Paramedic from the front seat gets slashed. The female paramedic backs off.

Intercutting between Melissa and The Pips, now racing to the crime scene.

The Driver slashes the female paramedic and moves viciously at Melissa on the table.

Six Pips vehicles bear down and surround the Paramedic Vehicle.

Billy Black and Redhead Girl close in on the Driver with pointed guns.

The Driver is persistently moving towards Melissa. Billy Black intercepts.

"Drop your weapon immediately, or we will shoot."

Peripherally, the Driver sees seven guns pointed in its direction.

However, it refrains from surrendering. Melissa is now closer to its reach than ever. The hoisted dagger is about to contact Melissa's upper body.
Multiple rounds from Billy Black and Redhead Girl's gun take down the resilient Driver.
Melissa flies into the arms of Redhead Girl.
A few blocks away, the Tow Truck is found slammed into a barrier, with its driver dead with a broken neck.

THE PIPS TEAM INVESTIGATES the remaining wreckage.
RADIOS TRANSMITS…

DISPATCH: Guys, all hell has broken loose in Brixton, London. A plane is waiting at Nice Cote d'Azur Airport.
"England? That's a Copy!"
Says Billy Black.
They HOTFOOT IT to their vehicles and motor off.

About The AUTHORS

John Alan Andrews hails from the islands of SVG in the Caribbean. He began his acting career in New York and took his craft to Hollywood in 1996. He appeared in multiple TV Ad campaigns and films, including John Q, starring Denzel Washington. Andrews later found his niche—writing coupled with filmmaking—and not only starred in but produced and directed some of his work, which won multiple awards in Hollywood.

With over 76 books in his multi-genre catalog, including **Rude Buay** poised for a Jamaican production, Andrews is currently drafting **The PIPS Series,** a police procedural TV series slated for the Mediterranean enclaves. He has also Co-Authored with his sons, **Jonathan Andrews** and **Jefferri Andrews.**

His latest books, Atomic Steps and Make Every Thought Pay You A Profit, are favorites among business leaders, and his twisted NYC Connivers legal thriller series appeals to both women and men ages 16 -85. The Pips Series (Body in a Suitcase). Also, Samuel A. Andrews—*Legacy* (A Biography).

His work can be found at **ALIPNET.COM** or **ALIPNET TV**, his recently launched OTT Streaming Platform.

John Alan Andrews states: "Some people create, while others compete. Creating is where the rubber meets the road. A dream worth having is one worth fighting for because freedom is not free; it carries a massive price tag."

VISIT: WWW.JOHNAANDREWS.COM

LIKE Us on FaceBook

https://www.facebook.com/Whoshotthesherifffilm

AUTHOR OF THE RUDE BUAY SERIES
JOHN A. ANDREWS
A MEMOIR IN TWO VOLUMES
HOW I RAISED MYSELF
FROM FAILURE TO
SUCCESS
IN HOLLYWOOD

INDIE SHORT FEST
AN AWARDS WINNER & MULTIPLE AWARD NOMINEE INDIE SHORT FILM
FEATURING
ANDREWS
PARKER
WALLERSON
CANTINE
RUDE
POIGNANT AND HARD HITTING...
PRESENTS AN UNCANNY PICTURES PRODUCTION
A BEST DIRECTOR & BEST CRIME SHORT AWARD WINNER

#1 International Bestselling Author
JOHN A. ANDREWS
THE UNTOUCHABLE
RUDE BUAY
An International Secret Service Agent Novel Series...

#1 INTERNATIONAL BESTSELLING AUTHOR
SHATTERPROOF
RUDE BUAY
JOHN A. ANDREWS

A COLLECTOR'S ITEM
JOHN A. ANDREWS
ACTION-
THRILLER
Series
RUDE
BUAY
VOLUMES 1-3

NACIONAL SUPERVENTAS
CHICO RUDO
THE UNSTOPPABLE
EL IMPARABLE
JOHN A. ANDREWS

SAUCE
02:29
A SUSPENSE MYSTERY HORROR
FROM THE CREATOR OF
RUDE BUAY
JOHN ALAN ANDREWS

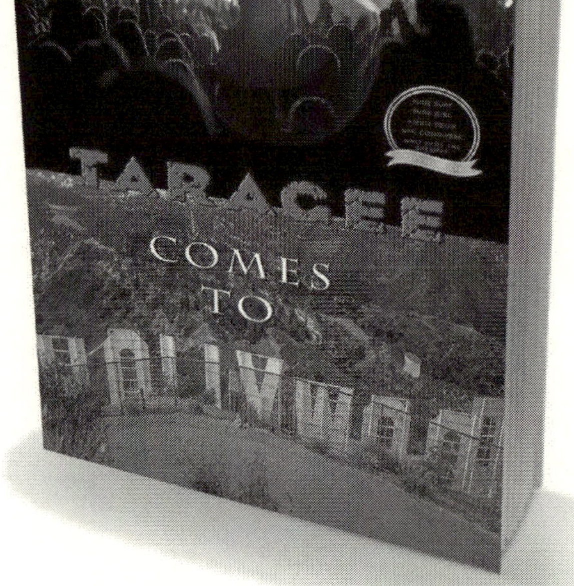
JOHN ALAN
ANDREWS
TARAGEE
COMES
TO

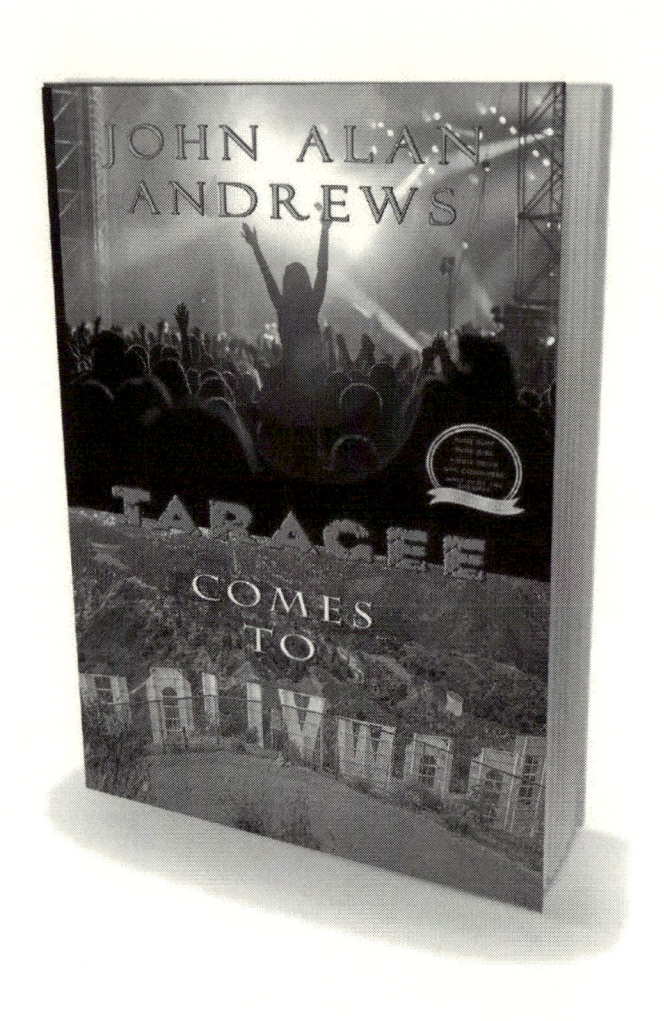

THE SOUL OF BLACK WALL STREET

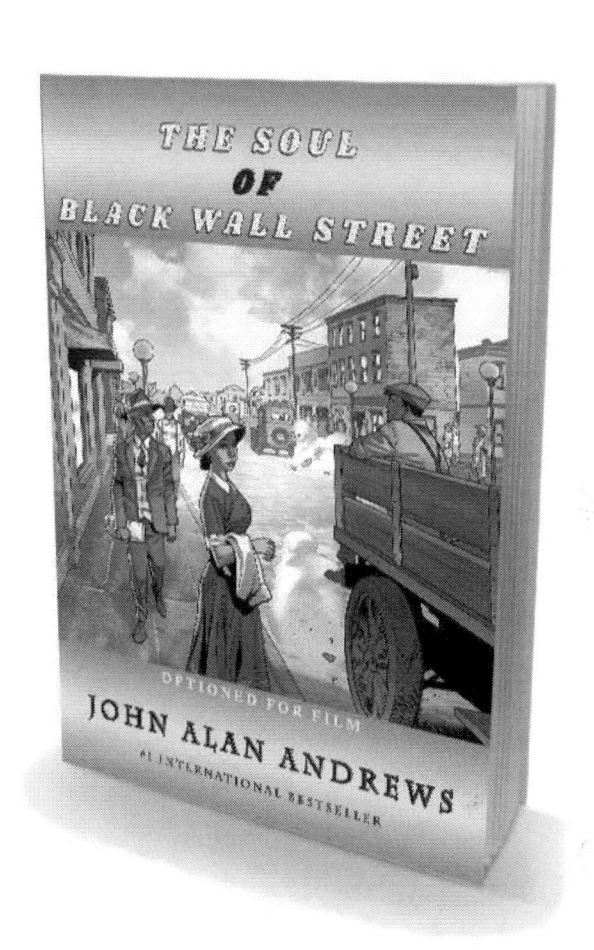

OPTIONED FOR FILM

JOHN ALAN ANDREWS

#1 INTERNATIONAL BESTSELLER

Climbing Up From The Bottom AUTHOR
JOHN A. ANDREWS
The 5 Steps To Changing Your Life
THE SUCCESS TRIANGLE™
Three Books In One Volume
Including DARE TO MAKE A DIFFERENCE

JOHN ALAN ANDREWS
AMBER BARBEE PICKENS
MOYA MONROQUE
A FIRST OUT OF THE GATE PANDEMIC FILM
San Francisco Indie Short Festival
Indie Short Fest
Indie Short Fest
BEST COVID FILM AWARD NOMINEE
Yearning To Exhale
TWENTY TWENTY LOCKDOWN
Global Shorts
Global Shorts
PG-13
UP
A BEST SCREENPLAY AWARD WINNER

ATOMIC
STEPS
WIN BIG OR GO HOME
WARNING: If you are determined to stay in your comfort zone. This book may not be for you.
INTERNATIONAL BESTSELLING AUTHOR
JOHN ALAN
ANDREWS

MAKE EVERY THOUGHT PAY YOU A PROFIT

JOHN ALAN ANDREWS

#1 INTERNATIONAL BESTSELLING AUTHOR OF
ATOMIC STEPS
WIN BIG OR GO HOME

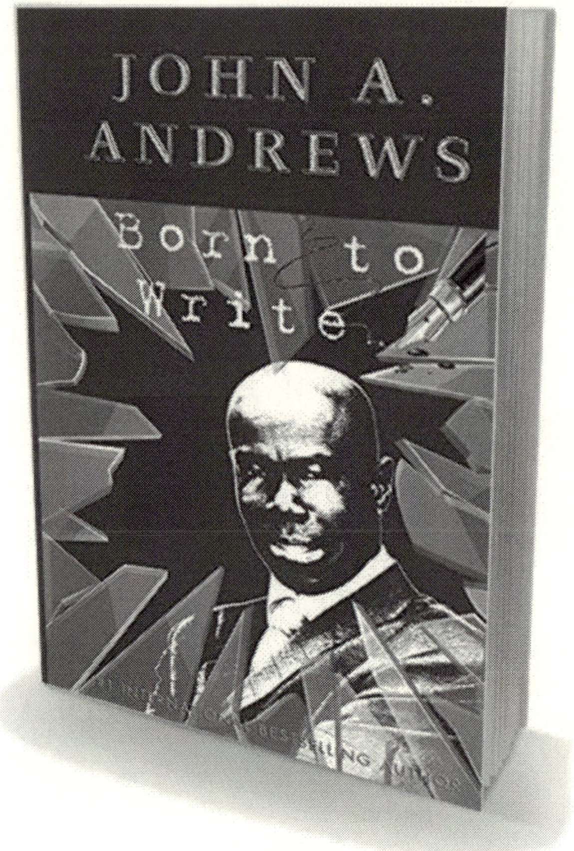
JOHN A.
ANDREWS
Born to
Write

DARE TO MAKE A DIFFERENCE
SUCCESS 101
FOR
ADULTS
#1 INTERNATIONAL BESTSELLING AUTHOR
JOHN A. ANDREWS

How I Wrote 8 Books In One Year
JOHN A.
ANDREWS
8
A
Author of
TOTAL COMMITTMENT
The Mindset Of Champions

By National Bestselling Author of Rude Buay ... The Unstoppable
TOTAL COMMITMENT
The Mindset of Champions
JOHN A. ANDREWS

DARE TO MAKE A DIFFERENCE
SUCCESS 101
FOR
ADULTS
#1 INTERNATIONAL BESTSELLING AUTHOR
JOHN A. ANDREWS

DARE TO MAKE
A DIFFERENCE
SUCCESS 101
FOR TEENS
JOHN A.
ANDREWS
#1 INTERNATIONAL BESTSELLING AUTHOR

ANDREWS
The FIVE
"Ps"
FOR TEENS

National Bestselling Author
John A. Andrews

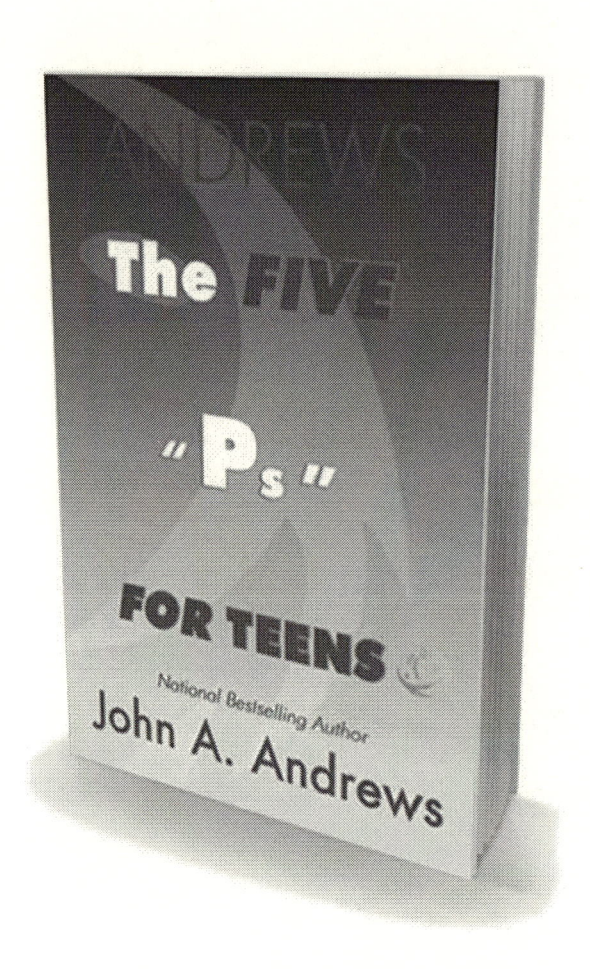

ANDREWS
John A. Andrews
Author of
How I Wrote 8-Books-In One Year™

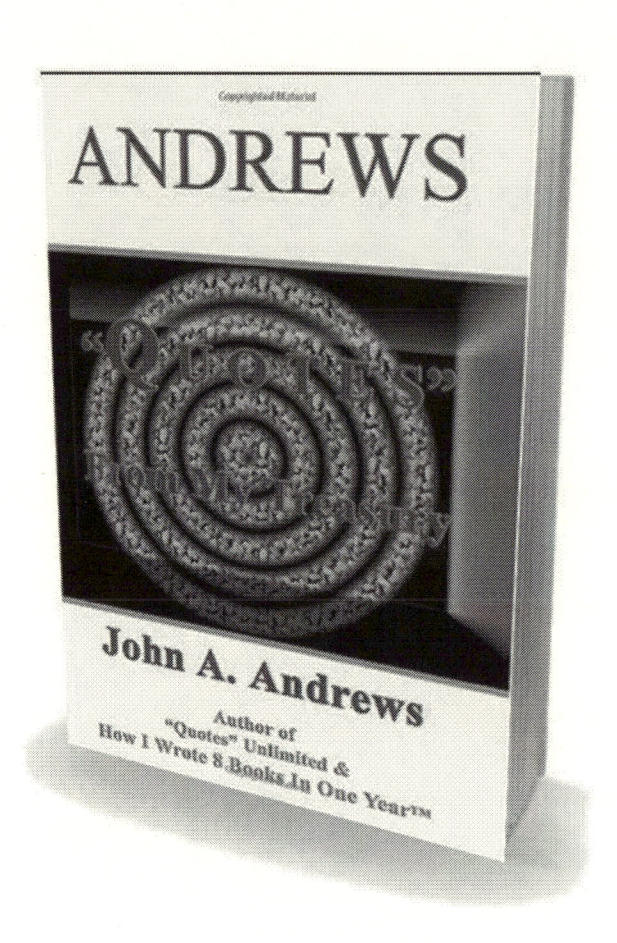

ANDREWS

"Quotes" from the Heart

John A. Andrews

Author of
"Quotes" Unlimited &
How I Wrote 8 Books In One Year™

ECLECTIC
QUOTES
SPEAK WITH
POWER
JOHN A.
ANDREWS
#1 INTERNATIONAL BESTSELLING AUTHOR

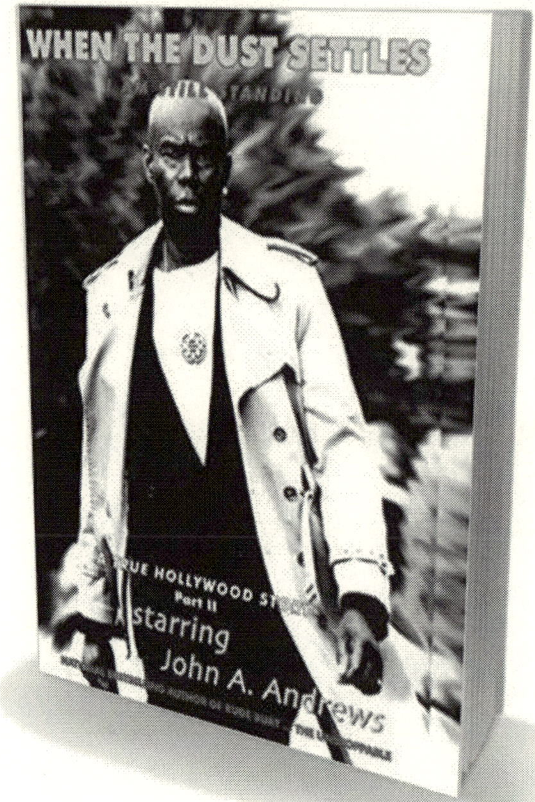
WHEN THE DUST SETTLES
Part II
starring
John A. Andrews

THE 5
STEPS TO
CHANGING
YOUR LIFE
BY: JOHN A. ANDREWS
"SEE YOU AT THE SUMMIT"

SHADES OF HER

BASED ON A TRUE HOLLYWOOD STORY

NYC
NEW YORK CONNIVERS ©
FROM THE CREATOR OF WHO SHOT THE SHERIFF?
JOHN A. ANDREWS
#1 INTERNATIONAL BESTSELLER
UNTIL DEATH DO US PART
A NOVEL
THE CRIME
THE COVER UP
THE CONCLUSION

NYC

NEW YORK CONNIVERS

FROM THE CREATOR OF WHO SHOT THE SHERIFF?

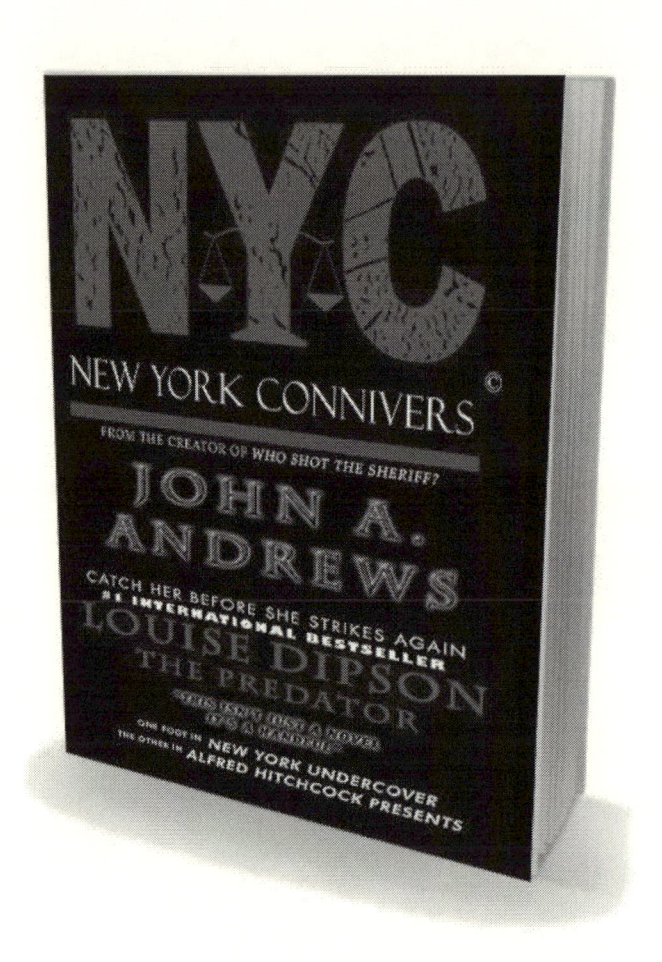

JOHN A. ANDREWS

CATCH HER BEFORE SHE STRIKES AGAIN
#1 INTERNATIONAL BESTSELLER

LOUISE DIPSON
THE PREDATOR

"THIS ISN'T JUST A NOVEL IT'S A HANDFUL"

ONE FOOT IN NEW YORK UNDERCOVER
THE OTHER IN ALFRED HITCHCOCK PRESENTS

NEW YORK CONNIVERS

FROM THE AUTHOR OF WHO SHOT THE SHERIFF?

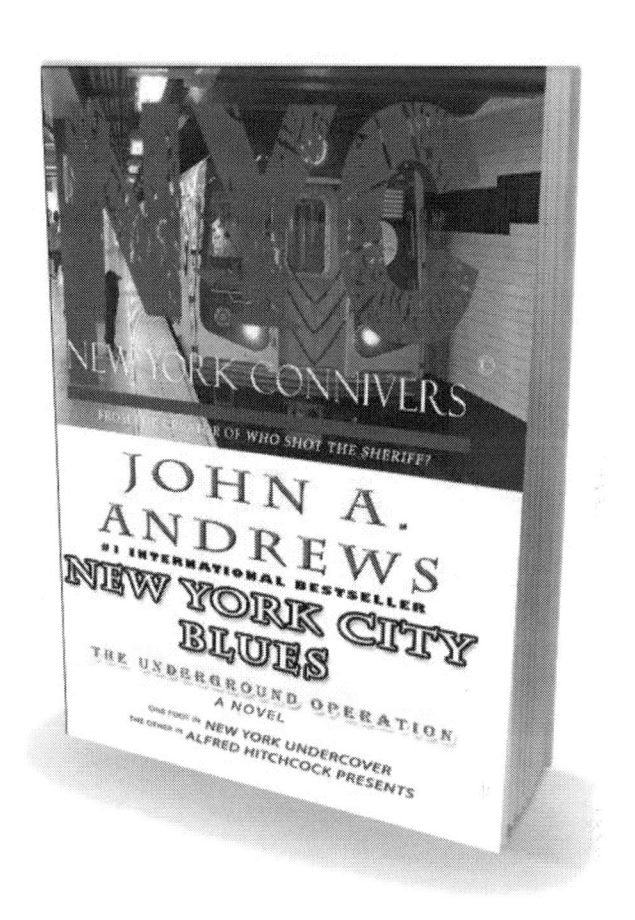

JOHN A. ANDREWS
#1 INTERNATIONAL BESTSELLER

NEW YORK CITY BLUES
THE UNDERGROUND OPERATION
A NOVEL

ONE FOOT IN **NEW YORK UNDERCOVER**
THE OTHER IN **ALFRED HITCHCOCK PRESENTS**

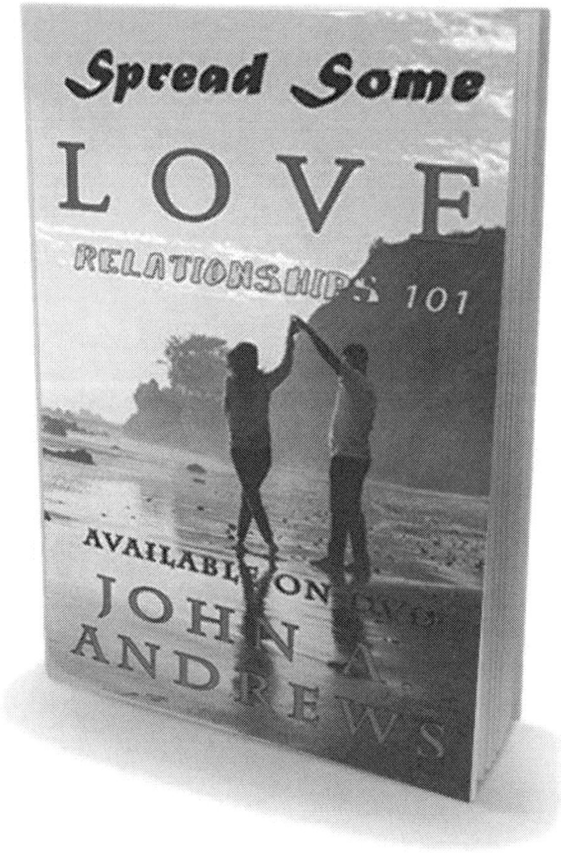
Spread Some
LOVE
RELATIONSHIPS 101
JOHN A.
ANDREWS

WHO SHOT
THE SHERIFF?
The Hustle, The Flow, The Verdict.
#1 INTERNATIONAL BESTSELLER
JOHN A.
ANDREWS

WHO SHOT
THE SHERIFF?
II
Let THE GAMES Begin...
The MILTON ROGERS' CONSPIRACY
JOHN A. ANDREWS
JONATHAN & JEFFERRI
ANDREWS

WHO SHOT
THE SHERIFF?
III
JOHN A.
ANDREWS
#1 INTERNATIONAL BESTSELLING AUTHOR
THE JURY
DEAD MEN TELL NO TALES
38

THE UNITED STATES PANDEMIC

FIGHTING THE INVISIBLE ENEMY

PANDEMIC WARFARE

JOHN A. ANDREWS

THE AFTERMATH OF COVID - 19

JOHN A. ANDREWS

The Church

IS IT A HOSPITAL?

THE MUSICAL®

FROM THE CREATOR OF
RUDE BUAY
THE WHODUNIT CHRONICLES
&
THE CHURCH ON FIRE

SO MANY ARE TRYING TO GO TO HEAVEN
WITHOUT FIRST BUILDING A HEAVEN
HERE ON EARTH...
#1 INTERNATIONAL BESTSELLER

THAT CONNECTS
PRAISE
HEAVEN & EARTH
FROM THE CREATOR OF
THE CHURCH...A HOSPITAL?
JOHN A. ANDREWS
THE
CHURCH
ON FIRE
THE MUSICAL®

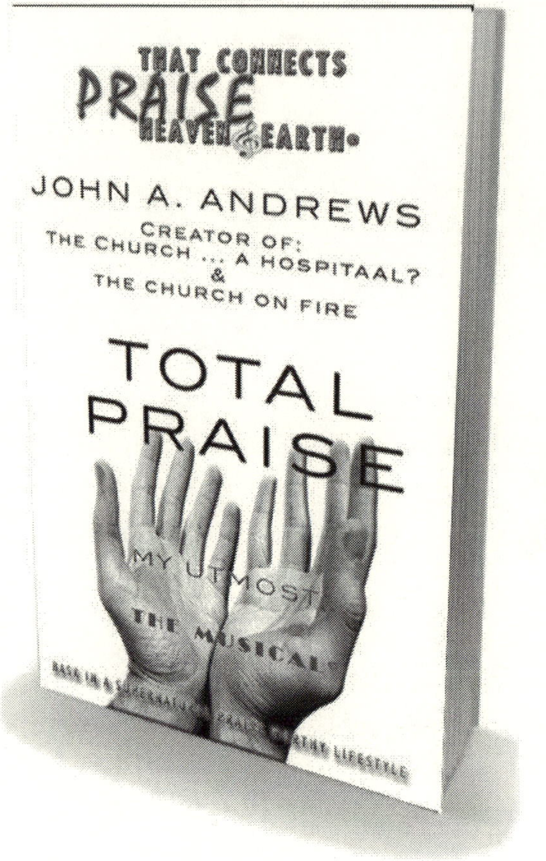
THAT CONNECTS
PRAISE
HEAVEN EARTH
JOHN A. ANDREWS
CREATOR OF:
THE CHURCH ... A HOSPITAAL?
&
THE CHURCH ON FIRE
TOTAL
PRAISE
MY UTMOST
THE MUSICAL

THE CHURCH RESTORED

THE CHURCH SERIES

THREE MUSICALS IN ONE VOLUME

JOHN A. ANDREWS

THE CHURCH – A HOSPITAL
THE CHURCH ON FIRE

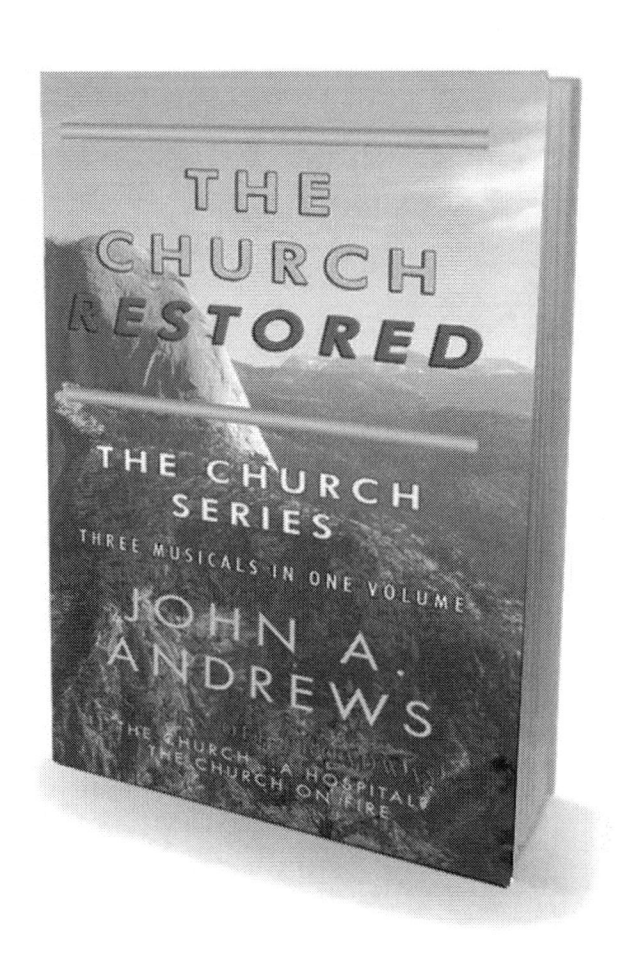

CROSS ATLANTIC FIASCO

A Riveting Novel

THREE EX-COPS, THEIR EX-BOSS, HIS 9 YEAR OLD DAUGHTER, AND THE BIGGEST BANK HEIST EVER ORCHESTRATED...

RENEGADE COPS

#1 INTERNATIONAL BESTSELLER

JOHN A. ANDREWS

Creator of
The RUDE BUAY Series
&
The WHODUNIT CHRONICLES

THE CARIBBEAN GETAWAYS

JOHN A. ANDREWS

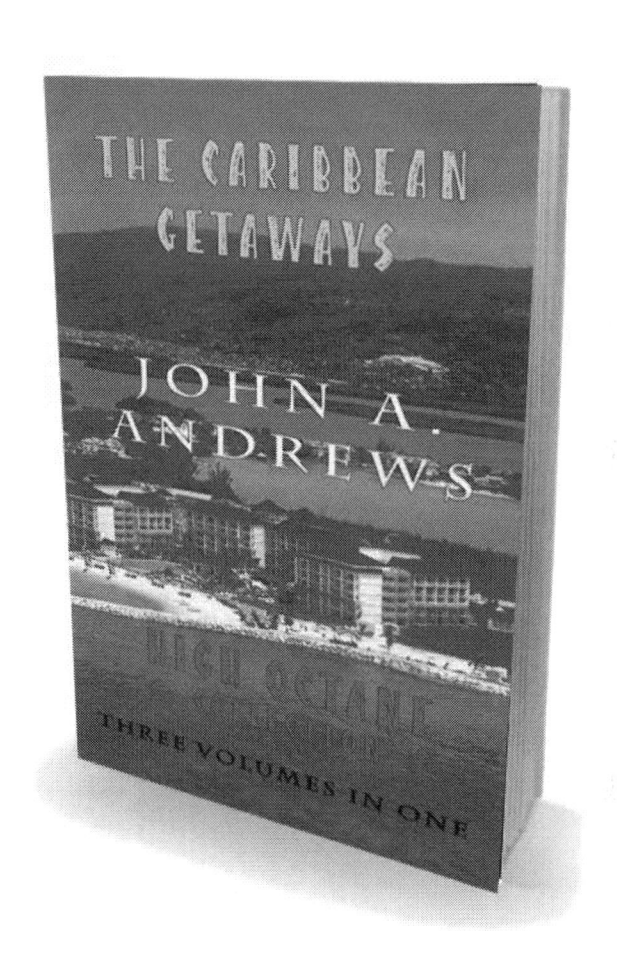

HIGH OCTANE

THREE VOLUMES IN ONE

THE BOTCHED
AMENDMENT
JOHN A.
ANDREWS
#1 INTERNATIONAL BESTSELLING AUTHOR
SUPPRESSING
THE BLACK VOTE

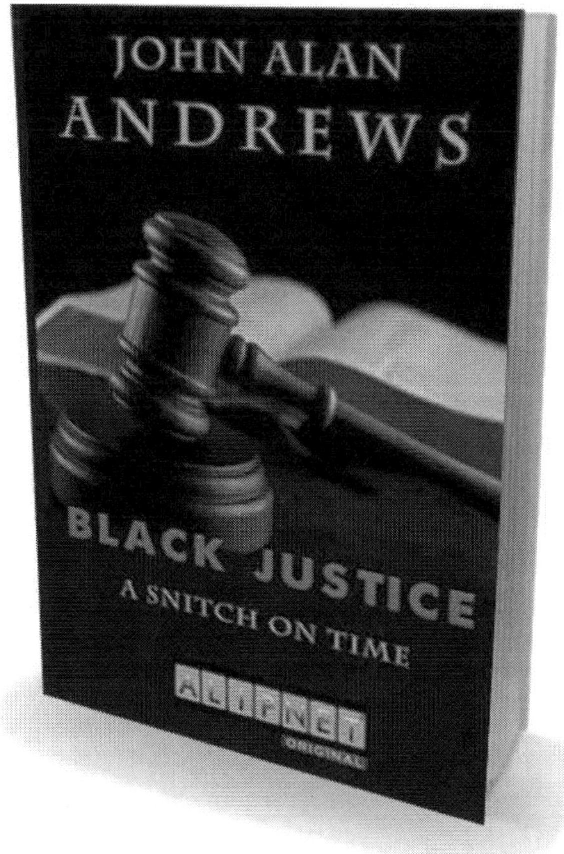
JOHN ALAN
ANDREWS
BLACK JUSTICE
A SNITCH ON TIME

JOHN & JONATHAN
ANDREWS

BLACK JUSTICE
INJUSTICE BAKED IN

CHASING DESTINY

GOT TO HAVE IT!

BASED ON THE NOVEL
A RUDE BUAY SIDEKICK
FROM THE CREATOR OF
RUDE BUAY

JOHN A. ANDREWS

RUDE GIRL

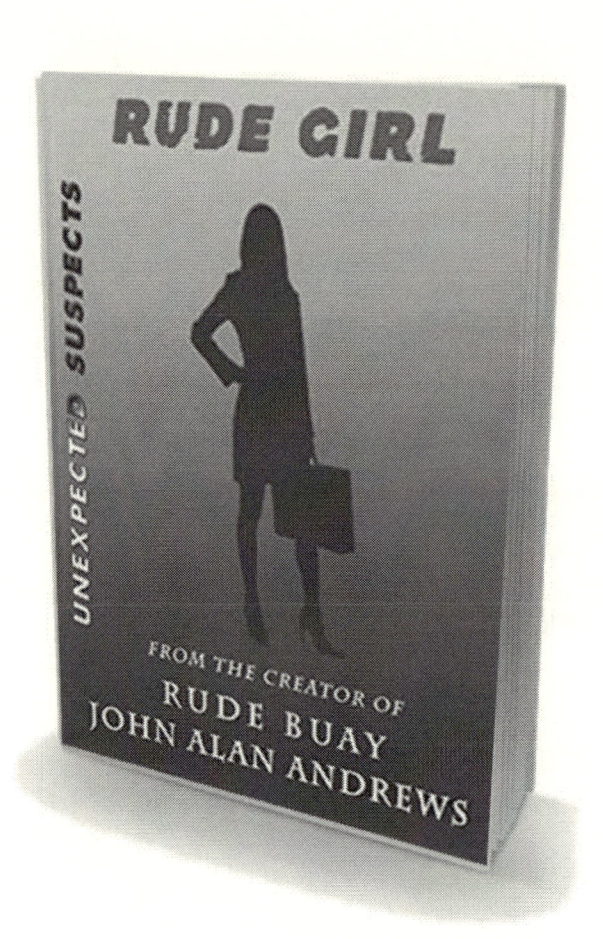

UNEXPECTED SUSPECTS

FROM THE CREATOR OF
RUDE BUAY
JOHN ALAN ANDREWS

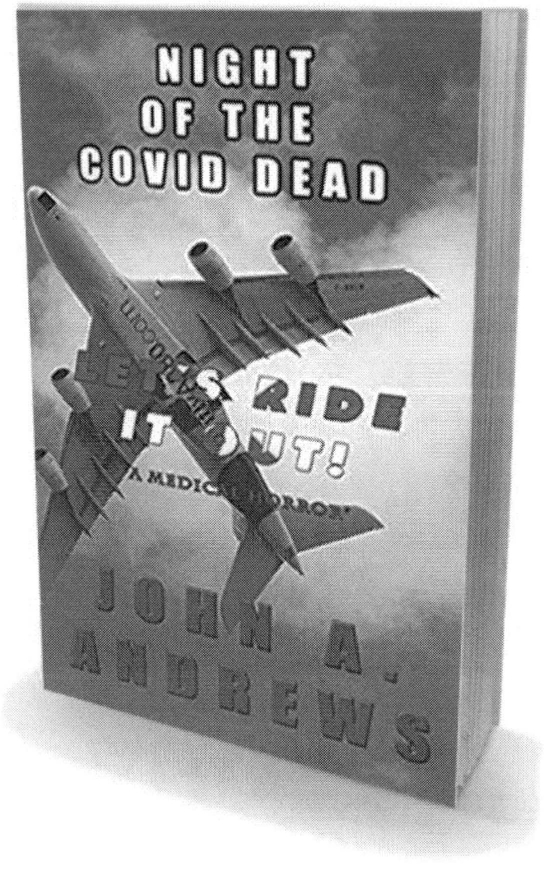
NIGHT
OF THE
COVID DEAD
LET'S RIDE
IT OUT!
A MEDICAL HORROR
JOHN A.
ANDREWS

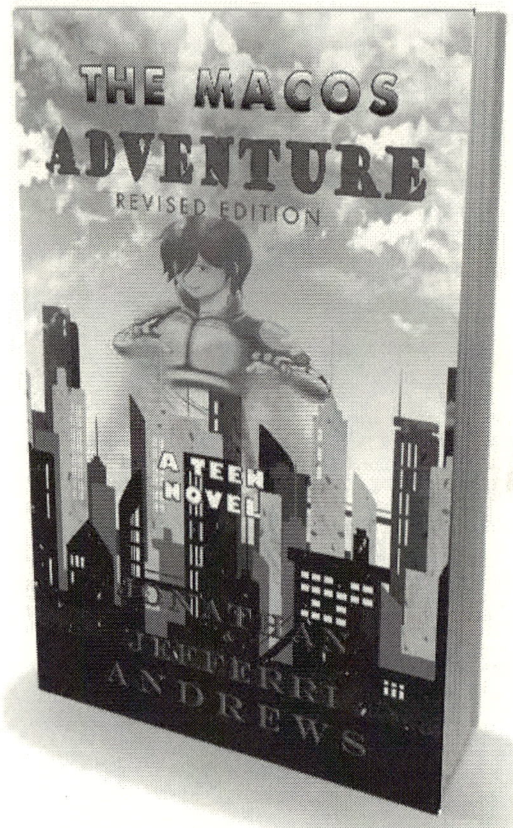
THE MACOS
ADVENTURE
REVISED EDITION
A TEEN NOVEL
ANDREWS

THE PIPS®

ALIPNET
ORIGINAL

WRITTEN BY
JOHN ALAN ANDREWS

CREATOR OF
RUDE BUAY

THE THUMB DRIVES

THE PIPS®
BODY IN
A SUITCASE
A PIPS SERIES NOVEL
#1 INTERNATIONAL BESTSELLING AUTHOR
JOHN ALAN
ANDREWS
CREATOR OF
RUDE BUAY

ALIPNET
ORIGINAL
THE PIPS®
MANHUNT IN PARADISE
WRITTEN BY
JOHN ALAN ANDREWS
CREATOR OF
RUDE BUAY

WHAT A MAN?
BIOGRAPHICAL
SAMUEL A. ANDREWS
LEGACY
BY
JOHN ALAN
ANDREWS

COMING SOON

THE MACOS
ADVENTURE
II
REVISED EDITION
THE AUTHORITY SQUAD
A TEEN NOVEL
JONATHAN
JEFFERRI
&
JOHN
ANDREWS

THE PIPS®

THE FRENCH CONNECT

WRITTEN BY
JOHN ALAN ANDREWS

CREATOR OF
RUDE BUAY ALIPNET
ORIGINAL

THE PIPS®

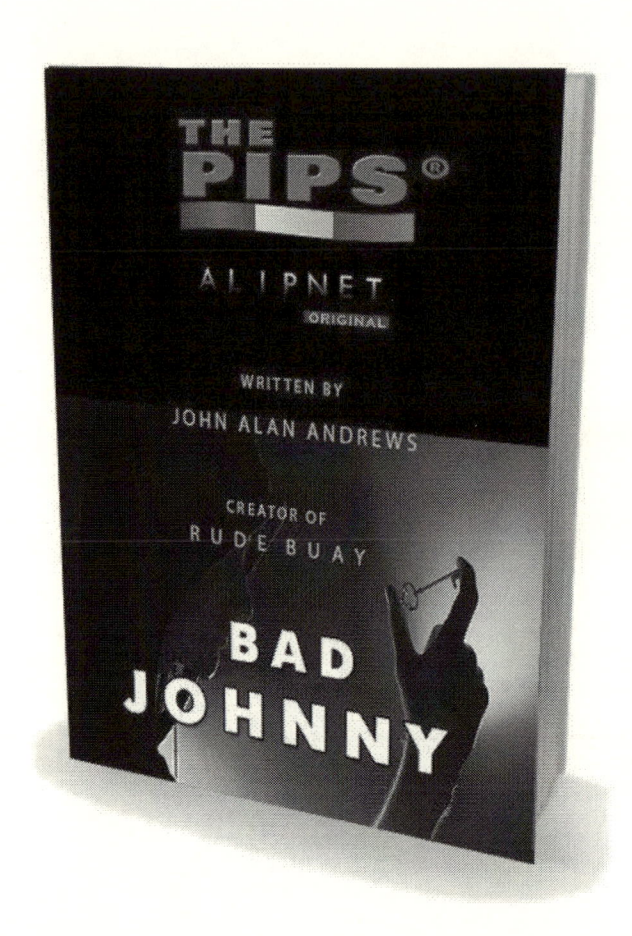

ALIPNET
ORIGINAL

WRITTEN BY
JOHN ALAN ANDREWS

CREATOR OF
RUDE BUAY

BAD JOHNNY

AI PNET
ORIGINAL

THE PIPS®

A PREDATOR IN PARADISE

WRITTEN BY
JOHN ALAN ANDREWS

CREATOR OF
RUDE BUAY

THE PIPS® 3IN1

MANHUNT IN PARADISE

BODY IN A SUITCASE

THE THUMB DRIVES

JOHN ALAN ANDREWS

"POOR EVENING MYSTERY LOVERS—WELCOME TO THE UNCANNY!"

#1 INTERNATIONAL BESTSELLING AUTHOR

BOOKS THAT WILL ENHANCE YOUR LIFE

ALIPNET
ORIGINAL